# BEST OF
# FRIENDS

Also by David Roth
*River Runaways*

# BEST OF FRIENDS

*by David Roth*

Houghton Mifflin Company    Boston    1983

*Library of Congress Cataloging in Publication Data*

Roth, David.
    Best of friends.

    Summary: While his parents vacation in Europe,
fifteen-year-old Matt falls in love with a "summer"
girl and discovers why his relationship with his older
brother has always been so poor.
    [1. Brothers—Fiction.    2. Family life—Fiction]
I. Title.
PZ7.R7275Be    1983          [Fic]          82-23378
ISBN  0-395-33889-1

Printed in the United States of America

V  10 9 8 7 6 5 4 3 2 1

This one is for Barry and Gretchen
— the very best of friends

# BEST OF
# FRIENDS

# Chapter 1

*T*he red of the bird was the first color he saw, and he immediately thought it was a scarlet tanager or perhaps a cardinal that had strayed too far north. But when he spotted it again in the top of a pitch pine, he realized the bird had a blue head and no high crest, so he ruled out a cardinal right away.

If the laces on his running shoes had been tied, he might have crept close enough for a better view of the bird. But he tripped instead, falling into the coarse grass that grew along the side of the dirt road. By the time he was up on his feet again, the bird was flying east, toward the lake. He managed to get his field glasses on the bird before it disappeared, and that was when he saw a flash of yellow on its wings.

He dropped his field glasses and looked down at the tattered laces that had tripped him. He tied them now that it was too late, then trotted along the dirt road in the direction the bird had taken.

Red breast, blue head, yellow on the wings . . . That didn't make any sense at all. He didn't have a guidebook with him, but he was sure he knew all the birds he might possibly see at this time of year around Lake Craddock. Red, blue, and yellow, all in one bird, was not among the possibilities.

Before he reached the lake he saw something moving through a grove of poplars. He cut down onto another dirt road and carefully approached the poplars, but the bird was only a goldfinch. He didn't get close enough to see whether it was male or female.

It was getting late, the shadows under the pitch pines beginning to spread together as the sun settled behind the ridge to the west. The pine barrens still held the heat of the day and he was still sweating from his pursuit of the strange new bird, but already a sense of evening was creeping into the woods. He did not care to go near the water now, and so he turned away and headed back toward his bike.

As he walked through the woods, taking first one narrow road then another, never hesitating in his choices, he ran one hand through his uncombed brown hair, something he did often when he was trying to think clearly. Right now he was trying to coax his brain into recalling a clear picture of the bird he had just seen. If he had a failing as an observer of birds — and he hated to admit even to himself that he did — it was that he tended to blur his recollections, so that if he was unable to get an exact identification in the field, by the time he got home and consulted his guidebooks he was no longer sure what he had seen.

Red, blue, and yellow . . . red breast, blue head, yellow on the wings . . . Remember it, he thought. Remember it.

His bike was leaning up against a small birch tree. He tied his shoelaces again and wheeled the bike toward the tarred road. He didn't want to go home, but it was getting too dark to see.

Red breast, blue head, yellow on the wings, he thought. Remember it . . .

There was a party at his house: a going-away barbecue for his parents, who were leaving for Europe tomorrow. His father had dragged out all the lawn furniture from the garage and borrowed more from the neighbors. The back yard was crowded with his parents' friends. He hopped off his bike and tried to wheel it, unnoticed, into the garage.

"Matthew!"

It was his mother. She was coming through the side door from the kitchen with a bowl of potato salad in her hands. He continued wheeling his bike into the garage.

"Matthew, it's about time you showed up. Everyone's been asking for you."

He doubted if even one person had asked, "Where's Matthew?" but he didn't say this to his mother. Instead he called out, "I was down in the pine barrens." He fiddled around in the garage, pretending his bike wouldn't stay leaning against the wall, but she was still there when he came out.

"You and those birds of yours," she said.

She wore a bright scarf tied around her summer-blonde hair. She always looked pretty for parties, he had to admit.

"Sometimes I think you care more about birds than you do people."

He shrugged. "You used to like bird watching."

She laughed. "That was a long time ago."

"Yeah, but you used to . . ."

She nodded her head toward the back yard. "Come on. Your father will be cooking the steaks soon."

He went into the kitchen and put his field glasses away in the closet. He drew himself a glass of water at the sink and drank slowly. Through the window over the sink he could see the festivities. At least twenty people were gathered around the patio with drinks in their hands. His father was hitting fly balls to John, who was circling around out there in the shadows by the back fence, catching them with ease. John, the natural athlete, big brother jock, Joe College now, showing off for all the . . .

"Matthew!"

He drank another glass of water. When he saw his mother coming around to get him, he went out.

"Here he is," said Mr. Bellows, his father's partner in the firm of Bellows and Zaharis, Real Estate for the Lake Region. "Your mother's been making excuses for you all afternoon."

His father paused from hitting fly balls to give him a sour look. "She's been making excuses for him for years."

Matt laughed. It was better to treat everything as a joke, when his father . . .

"Come on," John yelled from the far edge of the back yard. "Hit me another."

"Let Matt catch a few," his mother suggested.

He glared at her, but if she saw his look through the fading light, she ignored it. Having made the suggestion, she disowned it, turning to Mrs. Gannon and saying, "Let's light the torches before the mosquitoes get too thick."

His father tossed him a glove. "Go out and shag a few with your brother."

"It's too dark."

"Your brother isn't having any trouble catching them."

"John's got X-ray vision."

"Get."

Matthew put on the glove and trotted out toward the fence. John was standing out there by the crab apple tree, looking tanned and muscular in his cutoffs and tank top. The chain he wore around his neck glinted in the light from the orange sky. He claimed — to Matt at least — that the chain had been a gift from a married woman who . . .

"How are things in birdland?" John asked him.

"Ducky."

There was a crack from the bat and Matt turned around just in time to see a line drive rocketing toward him. He ducked and John speared the ball before it hit the fence.

"Nice move," John said.

"Thank you."

John tossed the ball in toward the patio. "I think he wanted you to catch that one."

"That's okay. Just call me generous."

"I call you a jerk," John told him.

"Whatever," Matt said. He went to the fence and

5

leaned against it, watching John catch one fly ball after another, even a high drive that would have cleared the fence by three feet if John hadn't vaulted up and snagged it at the last moment.

"I think you got potential," Matt yelled at him as he bounced down onto the lawn with the ball.

John grunted something unintelligible. Matt didn't ask him to repeat it.

"This one's for you, Matt," his father shouted. "If you don't catch it, you don't get your steak."

He was pretending to make it all sound like a joke, but Matt wasn't fooled. He heard the angry edge in his father's voice. It was time to make an effort.

"We'll feed it to the dog down the street," his father said as he tossed up the baseball and swung at it. Matt pushed away from the fence and punched the pocket of his glove, suddenly afraid.

It was always a question of not wanting to make a fool of himself and his father finding some way to make it happen. As he followed the course of the ball high up against the orange sky, he knew it was going to happen again. Even as he drifted off to his right, in perfect anticipation of the now-falling ball, he knew it was inevitable that he would . . .

He ran into the crab apple tree. As he fell, the ball bounced onto the ground two feet beyond his outstretched glove. He scrambled forward to retrieve it, thinking perhaps his father hadn't seen the ball hit the ground. Before he could reach it, John swooped in and plucked it up into his own glove.

"He blew it, Dad."

"So what else is new."

"Did you hurt yourself?" his mother called to him.

"No." He stood up, watching his brother trot in toward the patio with the ball held high. Mr. Olympian, carrying the torch.

"Are you sure you're all right, dear?" His mother was walking toward him. He wanted to run the other way.

"I'm fine," he said.

His father had tossed down the bat and was slamming steaks onto the grill, where they sizzled in noisy exuberance. Matt waited while the first batch cooked, talking with Mr. Bellows and another man about his plans for the summer. They didn't seem to think he had disgraced himself so badly that they shouldn't talk to him, but his father's back remained turned toward him even while the second batch of steaks cooked. Then he realized that one steak remained on the big steel platter, not cooking, naked in its pool of blood.

He didn't wait around for everyone to realize one steak hadn't been cooked, for his father to tell him to cook it himself. Before *that* happened, he slipped into the house.

He was leafing through the pages of his field guides, looking for something that resembled the multicolored bird he had seen in the pine barrens, when his mother came up to his room with his steak.

"Did *you* cook it?" he asked.

"Now what difference does it make," she said, smiling at him brightly, "whether I cooked it or your father did?"

If she didn't know, he wasn't going to try to explain it to her. He looked at the steak without appetite.

"You should eat it before it gets cold," she said. "It's a perfect medium, just the way you like it."

"Okay," he said, but he made no move toward it.

She looked at the books on his desk. "Couldn't you leave this for later and come out and . . ."

"I saw a really strange bird today," he told her. "I can't figure out what it was."

"That's nice."

"I want to identify it before I forget what it looked like. I want to put in my journal, and I can't just say . . ."

"We have company, dear."

"It's just a party."

"Isn't it a special party?" she asked. "After all, your father and I are going to be away for over a month."

He shrugged. "I suppose."

"Well, eat your steak," she said.

He pulled the plate across his desk and began cutting the meat. When he glanced at one of the guidebooks, she pulled them away and closed them all.

"Forget the birds for now." She tried a laugh. "My goodness, if I'd had any idea how obsessed you would someday be with them, I would never have gotten you started."

He chewed his way through one piece of steak and started on another. "It was really something today," he began. "This bird was . . ."

"Don't talk with your mouth full, dear." She was sitting on the edge of his bed, looking at her nails. "Will you be coming tomorrow to see us off?"

He shifted on his chair. "Well, I was planning to go up Firetop Mountain."

"Oh, Matt!" She took in a sharp breath and held it.

He looked at her. "I want to see if the ravens are . . ."

"We're going to be gone all summer, and all you can think about is ravens." She folded her hands in her lap as if to tidy up her emotions. "Besides, you know I don't like you going up on that mountain alone."

He looked down at his steak. "I was eight when I got lost up there. I'm almost sixteen now."

"Just the same, I want you to promise me that while your father and I are gone, you won't go up there alone."

"And who am I supposed to get to go up there with me?"

"I don't know, Matt, but I want you to promise." She stood up and came over to rub the back of his head. "Promise me you'll stay off that awful mountain."

"I won't go up there alone," he told her.

She kissed the top of his head "Good. And I expect you to come with us tomorrow to the airport. I don't think that's asking so very much."

He agreed finally, if only because he knew she would never let up until he did.

She took away his steak half-eaten. "Now come down and say good-night to everyone," she told him from the doorway. "They'll all be leaving soon."

He could hear his father laughing on the patio. John was shouting something that had set him off. Matt didn't go down. Instead, he reopened his bird books and continued the search for his mystery bird. Car doors were slamming in the driveway by the time he found it, but

9

"it" was impossible. His new sighting most closely resembled the picture of the painted bunting on page 210 of his best book. And painted buntings, according to this field guide, were southern birds. They never came within a thousand miles of Lake Craddock.

Well, he had seen it, hadn't he?

# Chapter 2

"Matthew? Are you coming?" His mother was at the foot of the stairs the next morning, calling him for the third time.

"Yeah, be right down." He was sitting at his desk, staring at the blank page in his journal that he had not filled in last night. It was important to write down his observations while they were still fresh.

"Matthew!" It was his father now, shouting from the driveway.

"Coming!" He dropped his pen and ran downstairs, nearly tripping on the untied laces of his running shoes. Outside, the top rack of the car was loaded with suitcases. John was already sitting behind the wheel; his father was climbing into the front beside him.

"Really, Matt, we're late enough without your making us later." His mother gave him a reproachful look as he joined her in the back of the car. "We were just going to leave without you."

"Sorry," he mumbled.

John winked at him as he leaned over the seat to back the car into the street. "Matt was probably hoping we'd leave him behind. Then he could go off spying on people with those field glasses of his." John laughed. "Maybe catch Mrs. Gannon taking a bath."

"John!"

"Well, you don't think he actually uses those glasses to look at birds, do you, Mom?" John gunned the car down the street and turned onto North Main at the corner. "He's the biggest peeping Tom in town."

"You know I don't like that sort of humor," she told John. "Maybe it's appreciated at your school, but when you're home, I wish you'd . . ."

John was laughing as they inched through the clogged streets in downtown Bredstone. Matt glared at him in the rearview mirror.

"Listen, little brother," John said as their eyes met, "I was up early enough the other day to see you aiming those glasses at Mrs. Gannon's upstairs windows."

"There was an eastern bluebird in her apple tree."

"Sure, Matt, sure."

"Okay you two, knock it off."

Matt watched his father search his pockets for his pipe, then exchange a look with John as he lit a match. John grinned and said something in a low voice that made his father laugh. Matt felt his neck burning and looked away, out the window of the car at the summer people milling around the outdoor stalls in front of Antonio's Market. His mother reached over and squeezed his hand, a special gesture that often passed between them.

"I'll send you a postcard the moment we get to London," she told him, as if that might make up for everything.

At the airport in Ellington the twin-engine plane that would take his parents to Boston was already loading passengers. There was barely enough time to check the baggage and then hurry outside onto the windswept asphalt apron between the small terminal building and the runway, where they said good-bye. Matt shook his father's hand and kissed his mother.

"Behave yourselves," Dad told them. "We'll call you Sunday."

"Don't worry," John said, glancing over at Matt. "He's in good hands."

"Take care of each other," Mom said. She looked as if she were going to cry. "Remember, Mrs. Gannon will be checking on you. If you need anything, just ask her. She's a good soul."

"Come on, dear, the plane will leave without us."

"If you need more money, John," Mom called as they hurried toward the waiting plane, "take it from your own account and we'll . . ."

The rest of her words were drowned out by the noise of the engines. It didn't matter; she had gone over every problem that might come up during her absence at least a dozen times. He and John and Dad had spent all spring convincing her that it would be safe for the two of them to go off to Europe this summer and leave Matt and John home alone. She stopped to wave one last time before stepping into the plane. To Matt it was clear that she was still not sure she was doing the right thing.

As the plane taxied down the runway he waved, then lingered there on the apron until the plane was only a silver glint in the sky, disappearing toward the south. John whacked him on his elbow.

"Come on, they can't see us anymore."

They walked back to the car. Matt was surprised to find that he already missed his parents. John guessed his feelings and grinned at him wickedly as he drove out of the parking lot.

"Mama's boy is going to have to grow up this summer," he said.

Matt glared at him but said nothing. They had never been friends, but now that John had spent his first year away at college, there seemed to be no common ground for them at all, no area of common interest left for them to share. Matt watched the outskirts of Ellington flash by as they headed back toward Bredstone. He glanced at John when he thought his brother wouldn't notice, wondering how well they would get on together, living alone in the house with no one to break up their quarrels.

John stepped down hard on the gas. He switched on the radio and found a loud rock station. He began to hit the steering wheel in time to the music.

"I think we'll have a party tonight, little brother," he said. "How does that sound to you?"

Matt shrugged.

John laughed. "Not that I really care what you think of the idea." He turned up the radio, then looked at Matt as if to dare him to try to turn it down. Matt looked away, out the open window at the passing farmland. The fields of young corn swept by in long, shifting rows. Matt tried

14

to look unconcerned with their speed, for he knew if John saw any sign of fear he would drive faster.

Matt thought about the plane that had flown away with his parents. It would be halfway to Boston already. He tried to imagine it now in that far distance, a small speck in the blue sky except when its windows caught the sun and flashed with reflected fire. In his mind it became a bird, flying south, and he longed to be with it.

Sometimes Matt believed that he and John were not brothers at all, they were so different. Even physically, he could see no similarity between them. John had their father's heavy build and dark hair. Matt had been blond until he was six or seven. Even now he still had such light brown hair that, like his mother's, it tended to bleach its way back toward blond every summer. He was thin like his mother, too, and given to the same long silences that upset people he was with, as if they did not trust his thoughts. John rarely shut up, it seemed to Matt.

When they were little, John had never tired of proving he was stronger. Not content with the edge that being three years older gave him, he had to prove he had some other, even more significant, advantage. The tide had run all John's way until Matt, when he was seven, had hit John in the head with a hammer while they struggled, silent and sweating, in the garage beside the house. Matt couldn't remember now what they had been fighting over that blinding-white day, but he could never forget how John looked, sprawled there on the cement floor, out cold.

Nor forget his fear that John was dead.

He had run to his mother and confessed everything, for

he had never been able to lie to her. He had sat beside her in the hospital waiting room, shedding contrite tears while John was examined for a possible skull fracture. No one knew that under the tears, under the guilt, under the fear, he was filled with wild elation for having gained the upper hand, if only briefly; for having finally paid his brother back for a dozen bloody noses, a hundred bruises, a thousand tormented days and nights.

After that John was more wary. He avoided direct attacks. He found other, more subtle ways to continue his campaign. If he had not been their father's favorite before this, he became his favorite now, and from this charmed position looked down at Matt as if to say, I'll always be first.

It was natural enough, then, for Matt to become his mother's son, and as a family they often found themselves divided along these lines. Sometimes Matt felt that he had lost a chance for something far more valuable than anything he had. For weeks at a time he would try in every way to gain his father's smiles and praise. Sometimes he would think he was succeeding, but John always found a way to force him out, to prove that when it came to choosing sides, their father would always choose sides with John.

When they got back to Bredstone, John parked the car as close to Antonio's Market as he could get. They walked the three blocks back to the store through crowds of summer people. Matt resented the tourists that flocked each summer into the area around Lake Craddock, turning Bredstone from a quiet small town into a miniature city.

In the market the crowding was even worse than on the street.

"What do we need?" Matt asked as they squeezed in between the bins of produce. He found himself jammed up against a display of watermelons.

"A case of beer, for one thing," John said, disappearing toward the back of the store.

Matt studied the watermelons until John came out with a case of beer on his shoulder. He pushed a grocery bag full of potato chips and pretzels into Matt's arms.

"How many people are you going to have over?" Matt asked him as they walked back to the car.

"Phil and Charlie, Michele, Nancy. Turk and Sonny from Waterford, if they can make it, with some girls from school, if Sonny can round them up." John opened the trunk and dropped the case of beer. "No way is this going to be enough," he said, and went back to Antonio's after another case.

Matt waited in the car, munching his way through a bag of pretzels. He watched in one of the side mirrors while John struggled to squeeze two more cases of beer into the trunk.

"This going to be a party?" he asked John when he slipped behind the wheel. "Or are you guys planning to swim in the stuff?"

John looked at him, then grabbed the pretzels. "Leave those for tonight, will you?"

"I only ate a few."

John closed the bag and pushed it back with the others. "Ate half the bag."

"So?"

"So leave them alone!" John jockeyed the car out of the tight parking place into the steady stream of traffic that was headed toward the lake.

"What am I supposed to do while you're having this party?"

John shrugged. "Join the human race and have some fun. Be real wild and invite some of your friends, if you have any."

Matt let the dig go by unanswered. "What about Mrs. Gannon?"

"What about her?" John leaned on the horn as traffic dragged to a halt. "Goddamn Burns really has things screwed up."

"What's Mrs. Gannon going to think when she sees us having a party the same day Mom and Dad leave?"

"What's she going to think?" John mimicked. "How the hell do I know? Maybe she'll be bent out of shape because we didn't invite her. Ask me if I give a damn."

John hit the horn again. Two blocks ahead August Burns, the town constable, was waving his arms, trying to get traffic moving again. Matt reached into the bag and stole another pretzel.

John glanced across at him. "Just tell your friends if they come to bring their own stuff to drink. That beer isn't going to last more than an hour or two as it is."

Matt knew that the beer had been charged against the grocery account their parents had left for them both. He was about to say something when John suddenly cut out of the traffic and shot up a narrow side street.

18

"Watch out!"

John jammed on the brakes and slid the car to a stop a couple of feet from the front end of a black Mercedes coming the other way.

Angrily, John tapped the horn several times, then held it down. "Go tell those summer jerks this is a one-way street."

Matt looked back. "There's a driveway right behind us."

"I'm not backing up for them!" John shouted. "Go on!"

Reluctantly, Matt got out of the car and walked slowly over to where the black Mercedes had stopped. He saw a plump, pretty girl sitting behind the wheel, an old man with thick white hair beside her. The girl's eyes were hidden behind dark glasses, but her face was flushed an angry red.

"What's the problem?" she demanded.

Matt pointed to the corner. "It's a one-way street."

"And I'm going the wrong way?" The girl's full lips twisted into a frown.

"I'm afraid so."

"And you can't back up into that driveway?"

"Well, my brother hates backing up."

She took off her glasses and stared at him. Her eyes were dark brown and enormous. "I'll have to back up for a whole block."

John was pounding the horn again. Matt waved at him to stop, but he didn't. "I'm sorry," Matt said. "He's just not going to budge."

"What kind of weird slobs are you two, anyway?"

Matt felt his face beginning to burn. He shrugged.

19

"Just your average, run-of-the-mill, everyday kind," he told her.

The old man sitting beside the girl reached over and tapped her arm. "Back up the car," he told her. He did not look at Matt. "Back up the car, Andy," he said again.

The girl glared at Matt and jammed her sunglasses back on. She said something under her breath.

"I'm sorry," Matt told her again.

"Yeah, I bet." She shifted gears and floored the accelerator, sending the Mercedes squealing back toward the other end of the street. As Matt climbed in beside John he heard metal scraping in the distance, and the sound of breaking glass.

John slowed down as they passed the corner. The girl had backed in too close to a stone wall, running the Mercedes up against it.

"You ought to stop," Matt said.

John shook his head. "It has nothing to do with us if she can't drive that thing." He stepped on the gas.

Looking back, Matt saw the girl, who was out of her car, turn toward them as they drove by.

"Did she just do what I think she did?" John asked.

"Yeah, she did. Twice. Once for you, once for me."

John laughed. "Nasty girl."

Matt wanted to laugh with him. What had happened was certainly funny enough to deserve at least a smile. But he couldn't laugh and he didn't smile. Instead, he remembered the girl's dark and luminous eyes and felt guilty, as if he had disappointed her, a perfect stranger.

# Chapter 3

John's friends began arriving for the party after eight, and by nine o'clock the house was full. Matt knew Phil and Charlie, Michele and Nancy — John's friends from high school, who were also back in Bredstone for the summer. He talked with Charlie briefly as he drifted through the living room. Michele made a big show of telling him what a cute little heartbreaker he was growing up to be and the girls of Bredstone had better watch out, he might even break his big brother's record by the time he finished high school. Matt didn't ask her what record that was, but he could guess.

"What are you up to this summer?" Michele asked, then turned away to talk to someone else before he could tell her.

"I'm bird watching a lot," he told her anyway. He went into the kitchen to get himself a beer before they all disappeared.

Most of the people arriving late at the party were John's

friends from college: loud-mouthed jocks clutching half-empty fifths of whiskey. The girls they brought with them poked around the house as if they were on a scavenger hunt.

"Strange books," one of them said when he came upon her emptying the shelves out on the porch. "Who reads *these?*"

"My father did, before he went senile," Matt told her. "Watch out, he's got one of them rigged to explode. We never could figure out which one and he won't tell."

She looked at him. "You're kidding."

He nodded. "Of course I am. Would you like to take them with you? We can give you a good price. Most everything in the house is for sale. Dad's been running up some pretty terrible medical bills."

She backed away from him, a faint smile on her lips. When she was gone, he knelt down and replaced the books on the shelves. John stuck his head out the living room door and yelled at him.

"Cool it, Matt."

"What?"

"Just don't go weird right now, okay?"

"Anything you say." Matt followed him back into the living room and flicked the wall switch off and on twice. "Who wants to see the slides from Yosemite?" he shouted above the noise of a dozen conversations. Before John could reach him, he ducked into the kitchen, where he put on an apron and baked a batch of chocolate chip cookies from a package of frozen dough he found in the freezer. John pretended not to see him when he came out, still wearing the apron, to pass the cookies around.

"These are good!" Michele squealed as she bit into one.

Matt nodded, holding the tray out to Nancy. "It's an old family recipe and I've promised John I won't give it to anyone."

He insisted Nancy take a cookie. She was looking at him as if he had just come out from under a rock. He couldn't stop now, even though he knew he should. "John really does love his cookies," he told them.

Michele reached out and pinched his cheek. "You're too much, you know that?"

He backed away from them and headed toward John, the tray of cookies held high over his head. "Don't worry, Johnny, I've saved some for you."

His brother rushed to meet him and knocked the tray flying, scattering the remaining cookies in all directions. The tray landed with a clatter on top of the television.

"Stop it!" John yelled. "Act weird somewhere else!"

A group of summer kids pushed in through the front door, carrying another case of beer. Matt used this diversion to cover his retreat to the kitchen, picking up the broken cookies as he went. Michele tried to follow him. He avoided her by continuing through the kitchen and out the side door.

"You still have the apron on," she called to him from the doorway.

He pulled it off and draped it over a rose bush.

"Where are you going?"

"For a walk."

"Want some company?"

"No."

Two blocks away he could still hear the party behind

him, the laughter and the music floating through the soft summer air. As he passed Mrs. Gannon's house, he saw her standing behind one window blind, peering out. He waved, but she didn't see him.

He walked to the lake and sat down on one of the boulders that separated the parking lot from the town beach. Small waves were breaking on the sand, and the wind smelled of the water. On the far shore a line of lights marked the road that skirted the pine barrens.

What drew him to the lake at times like this when he needed to be alone he wasn't sure, except that he knew it had something to do with the fact that he both feared and loved the water. He could never go into it, yet it seemed to represent to him all the things he longed for. The beach, which he would never go near during the day when it was crowded with swimmers, became something else for him at night, when it was empty. It was *his* beach then, a place where he could come and look across at distant lights.

He stood up and walked to the edge of the lake, thinking that someday he would just walk into the water and no longer be afraid. But not tonight. He stopped with the toes of his running shoes just touching the last ripples of the little waves. Not tonight . . .

He turned away from the water when headlights swept over him. The town police car was pulling into the parking lot. It slid to a stop on the sandy asphalt.

"Who's that down there?"

Matt walked off the beach toward the police car. August Burns was hanging out his door, watching him.

"You're the Zaharis boy, right?"

Matt nodded.

"Out by yourself?" August Burns scratched his whiskery face.

"Yeah, just walking."

August Burns sat down behind the wheel of the car. "Well, be careful on the road. You're dressed kind of dark."

"I will." Matt watched him drive off, the radio blaring gibberish as the police car reached the road. August Burns had his blue lights flashing before he reached the intersection. He turned south.

Matt hoped he was rushing off to break up John's party. Maybe one of the neighbors had complained, maybe Mrs. Gannon.

But he wasn't so lucky. Everything was going full blast when he got home.

He opened another beer for himself as he came through the kitchen, then turned on the television in the side room and sat down a few feet in front of the set to watch the actors' mouths move through the lines of an old western.

It was Michele who suggested they all go for a swim. The idea caught fire and soon everyone was racing outside with the last of the beer, the last of the whiskey, squeezing into cars whether they knew the person driving or not. He walked onto the front porch to watch them go.

"Come on, Matt," Michele shouted to him. "Come for a swim with us."

He shook his head. "No thanks."

"Oh, come on. I'll teach you the breast stroke." She

giggled and leaned against John, who was struggling to get the car keys out of his pocket.

"No, it's too chilly tonight," Matt lied. "Go on, have fun."

Michele wasn't listening to his excuses. She started toward the house as the last two cars squealed off toward the lake. John grabbed her arm and pulled her back.

"Forget it. He won't come. He's scared of the water, remember?"

"But I can help him," she argued. "It's time he learned how to swim." She looked up to where Matt stood in the doorway, not moving. "Isn't it, Matty? Isn't it time somebody taught you how to swim?"

"Not tonight," he said in a low voice.

"What?"

"Come on, Michele," John told her.

"Not without Matt."

"I told you, he's too scared to learn how to swim. He won't even put his feet in the water."

She allowed John to push her into the car. Matt watched them drive off after the others. As silence slowly filtered back into the street, he became conscious of the moths beating against the outside light. He closed the door and looked at the shambles of the living room. He walked slowly through the house, looking around him as if he expected to find a stray guest or two lying under a chair or asleep in a dark corner.

He was in the kitchen washing glasses when someone tapped on the side door. He opened it to find Mrs.

Gannon standing there, a sweater gathered around her shoulders.

"Matthew," she said, looking past him into the kitchen, "I don't mean to intrude, but . . ."

"They've all gone for a swim," he told her.

"Is everything all right?"

"Sure." He didn't invite her inside. He didn't want her to see the mess in the other rooms.

"Well, your mother did ask me to . . ." Mrs. Gannon pulled the sweater more tightly around her shoulders. Her face wrinkled up in a frown. "Not to spy, just to be of help if I can."

He nodded. "She told me to be sure to let you know if we need anything. They were both really excited about the trip."

Mrs. Gannon's face brightened. With the frown gone, she no longer looked old enough to be his grandmother. "Did they get off all right?"

"Far as I know. They flew into Boston from Ellington. I think they were expecting a two-hour wait for their flight to London."

She backed down a step. "Will they be calling you soon?"

"Sunday."

"Well, be sure to give them my best. I hope they have a good time."

"I will, Mrs. Gannon." He started to close the door.

"You're sure everything's all right over here tonight?"

"Just fine," he told her. "Just a little party for some of John's friends."

"And your mother knew about it?"

"Told her all about it before they left."

"All right, Matt. Good-night."

"Good-night, Mrs. Gannon."

He returned to the living room and gathered up the rest of the dirty glasses. When they were all washed, he decided that this was his share of the cleanup chores and went up to his bedroom.

His journal lay open on his desk where he had left it that morning. He remembered now the bird he had spotted yesterday afternoon, the one that resembled a painted bunting. The memory of the sighting was badly faded now. He leafed through the pages of his best field guide, found the picture of the painted bunting, studied it carefully, trying to match it to his fading recollections of the bird he had seen. If his bird wasn't a painted bunting, what was it?

He closed the book and reached for the journal. He was keeping it for Mr. Doninger, the only teacher he liked at Bredstone High. He wrote his entry in a neat, precise hand — the hand of a budding scientist, he sometimes thought:

*July 15*

*Observations yesterday included a flock of red-winged blackbirds, a pair of purple finches, an American goldfinch. I heard a nuthatch but didn't get a look, so I couldn't tell if it was white-breasted or red. And, of course, there were the usual bossy blue jays.*

He hesitated. He was torn between two needs: his

desire to keep this journal accurate and truthful, and his reluctance to appear foolish. To write down here, for Mr. Doninger to read later, that he thought he had seen a painted bunting would be almost as risky as telling people about the raven up on Firetop Mountain that had rescued him when he was eight years old. But if the journal was to be of any value at all, it had to contain every observation he made all summer. He plunged on:

> *I saw for just a few seconds, a very color-ful bird about the size of a purple finch, maybe a little smaller. It was hiding in a sumac grove, then darted to the top of a pitch pine. When I tried to get close, it flew away toward the lake.*
>
> *I cannot identify it; it most resembles the picture of the painted bunting in one of my books, but that's impossible, since these buntings are limited to the south. Could it be an escaped pet bird?*

Matt nibbled on the end of his pen, then added:

> *If it is, I pity it come winter.*

He read over what he had written, then put the journal away in the top drawer of his desk. This was his only attempt at order. The top of his desk was a clutter of books, pamphlets, and maps. Above the desk a U.S. Geological Survey map of Lake Craddock and its surroundings was taped to the wall. Beside it, on a shelf, was his prized collection of stuffed birds. The cornerstone of his

29

collection was a great horned owl that Mr. Doninger had given him last year.

The owl seemed to watch every corner of the room from its perch on the shelf. His mother hated it. She had made several attempts to bribe him into throwing the owl away, or at least hiding it in his closet. But he had not given in to her wishes.

"I don't know what gets into you sometimes," his mother was fond of saying lately. But she did not try to take the owl away without his permission.

He searched through the books on the floor, found the one he was currently reading, then curled up on top of his bed to continue following two adventurers as they traveled by canoe across a chain of Canadian lakes. He was dimly aware of John's return with some of the others from their swim. The party resumed, but more quietly now, the stereo not shaking the walls, the conversation only a low, faraway murmur. Matt fell asleep with his light on.

He woke up from a dream of the cold, green Canadian lakes to hear someone giggling near his bed. Opening his eyes, he saw Michele and Nancy peering down at him.

"What's going on?" he mumbled, still trying to shake off the thick layers of sleep.

"Sssh!" Michele hissed at him. "You'll wake him up."

"Wake who up?"

"Matt." She started to sit on the edge of his bed, but fell onto the floor instead. Nancy, giggling so much she could hardly stand up herself, tried to help her to her feet.

"Know what?" Matt said, rubbing his face and looking at them, now that he could focus his eyes.

"What?" Nancy asked. She managed to get Michele onto her feet, but the effort sent her staggering back against his desk, knocking his chair over on its side.

"You're both wet and full of sand and drunk, and I wish you'd get out of my room."

Michele perched precariously on his bed and blew her breath into his face. "What makes you think we're drunk?"

"Just a wild guess." The side door slammed downstairs, and John shouted to someone in the yard.

"We can't go yet," Michele told him. "We have a mission."

Matt looked at her. Something warned him not to ask, but she went ahead and told him anyway.

"We have been sent," she said, holding up one finger to keep his attention, "to seduce you, against your will if necessary. Haven't we, Nan?"

"What?"

"Been sent to seduce this poor, unfortunate boy, this poor, poor, virgin boy?"

Nancy sat down on his desk. Leaning back, she pushed a pile of books and maps onto the floor. "We sure have, Michele, and it looks like an uphill battle to me." She stared at Matt as if he were a side of beef she had to cut up with a dull knife. "Look, he even sleeps in his clothes."

"I know," Michele said, trying to pull Matt's shirt open, managing only to pop off one button. "Most uncooperative."

He pushed her hands away. "Why don't you two get lost?"

"No way, Matty dear. Your time has come."

He climbed off the bed and ducked away from her.

Nancy snatched the owl from the shelf and hit him over the head with it, sending feathers around him in a cloud.

"Leave that alone!" he shouted.

But she was swinging at him again, trying to drive him back toward the bed. One of the owl's wings was bent at an unnatural angle.

"Owl power!" Michele shouted behind him. "Get him, Nan."

He grabbed the owl out of Nancy's hands and clutched it against his chest. Feathers continued to drift down around him. "Get out of here," he told them. Fury made his words come out in a harsh squawk. He pushed Nancy toward the door. "Get out!"

Nancy jumped out of his way, slapping at his hands as if she were suddenly afraid of what he would do if he grabbed hold of her.

"Let's go," Michele said. "He's hopeless." At the doorway she stopped to look at him. "We were only having some fun, doing John a favor."

He was still holding the owl tightly. "I don't need John picking out girls for me."

They went down the stairs together. "You need something!" Nancy shouted back at him.

He stood there long after they were gone, still holding the owl, hearing their laughter downstairs as they told John what had happened. "Go to hell," he whispered. "All of you, go to hell."

He tried to clean up the feathers, but they scattered all the more as he chased after them.

The owl, returned to its perch on the shelf beside the other stuffed birds, regarded him with a wounded look. The damaged wing refused to tuck back where it belonged.

Unable to sleep, Matt read for hours. Occasionally sounds from below drifted up to him, and he was aware of people leaving, cars driving off into the night. When at last the house was quiet, he heard John walking through the rooms, picking up empty bottles, dropping them into the trash in the kitchen.

He read on, finishing one book, starting another. At four o'clock, when John opened his bedroom door and looked in at him, Matt was still awake.

John shook his head. "There's no saving you, you know that, Matt?"

Matt looked at him but said nothing. Finally John closed his door and walked across the hall to his own room.

# Chapter 4

The next morning at breakfast John was too hung over to say much. They had both slept late. They ate in the kitchen at one end of the cluttered table. Matt had his face buried in a wildlife magazine and was surprised when John touched his arm.

"I want to talk to you," he said in a low voice.

Matt put down the magazine. "Go."

"I think we should come to an understanding."

"About what?"

"About this summer. About us." John got up and went to the stove after a second cup of coffee.

"What about us?" Matt asked. His eyes strayed back to the magazine.

"Live and let live, that's what I say."

"So did someone else, I think."

"Look, knock off the wise remarks for once, will you?" John sat down again and looked into his coffee cup. "You go your way this summer and I'll go mine."

"Suits me."

"I mean, there's no reason for us to do things together."

"Right."

"It's not like we have any interests in common, or . . ."

"I know."

John looked up. "I know I'm supposed to keep an eye on you while Mom and Dad are gone."

Matt felt his face flush. "I can look after myself."

"Okay, then you agree?"

Matt nodded.

John seemed relieved. He sat back in his chair and sipped his coffee. "So except for painting the house, you do what you want to do and I'll do what I want."

"Fine with me." Matt took his dishes to the sink and rinsed them. "When do we start the painting?"

"No rush. We promised Dad we'd have it done by the time they get back. We have plenty of time."

"Okay." Matt went to the closet for his field glasses. "See you around."

"Wait a second." John got up from the table and tried to head him off before he could reach the side door. "Aren't you going to help me clean up this mess?"

Matt reached the door ahead of him and slipped outside. "I cleaned up my share last night."

"Hardly."

"Hey, John, your friends made that mess. You clean it up." He took his ten-speed out of the garage and slung the strap of the field glasses over his shoulder before heading down the driveway.

"Thanks, you little jerk," John called as he rode away.

"Don't mention it," Matt shouted back.

As he rode by the lake, he could see the crowd of sun-bathers and swimmers on the town beach. He took the street that ran along the south side of the lake, where the cottages were all full, all displaying No Vacancy signs.

A late-morning haze hung over the water. The sky overhead was pale blue. It was already too late and too hot for the birds to be at their liveliest in the pine barrens.

But that was where he was going. He would put off his planned visit to Firetop Mountain. It was too hot today to go climbing up there.

In the barrens he could hope for another sighting of the strange, multicolored bird. The promise his mother had bullied out of him the night before she left wasn't keeping him off the mountain.

At least he didn't think so . . .

Where the shoreline of the lake swung away to the north, he left the tarred road and bounced onto a sandy track that led in among the pitch pines and the poplars. He left his bike at the edge of the barrens and walked in, following the crisscrossing dirt roads at random.

It was close to the sleepy noon hour. He could smell the pines and the warm, sandy soil. As he came closer to the shore, he caught the scent of the water itself: cool, moist, fragrant. Other than a flock of chickadees that followed him, darting from tree to tree along the road as he walked toward the lake, he saw no birds.

At the edge of the woods, above the rock shore of the lake, he raised his field glasses and searched the islands. A lone gull was soaring high above the largest island, but he could not tell if it was a herring gull or a ring-billed gull. Lake Craddock was large enough to support its own population of gulls.

"Do you see anything out there?"

He whirled around to look, then recognized the girl who had been driving the black Mercedes yesterday. He remembered her large brown eyes, her full lips.

She recognized him, too, and the smile on her lips faded. "Oh, it's you," she said.

"Yeah," he said. She had a pair of field glasses draped on a strap around her neck, and this gave him the courage he needed to stay there and face her. "It's me." He nodded toward the offshore islands. "Nothing out there except one lonesome gull." When she said nothing, he struggled on. "I haven't seen much today. It's too late, too close to noon."

She glanced at her watch. "It *is* noon. I've been out for hours." Then she shook her head. "I don't know why I'm even talking to you. It's your fault I banged up the car."

She was not as old as he had first thought. Away from the Mercedes, she looked smaller, younger, less sure of herself.

"That was my brother's fault," he said. "I was just delivering his message."

"Do you always do your brother's dirty work?"

"No more than I can help."

She pushed her dark hair back from her face. Her eyes did not waver as they studied him; he could not avoid looking into them, unless he turned away.

"No more than I can help," he said again.

Suddenly she laughed. "Why don't you say you're sorry and I'll say it's okay and then we'll be done with the whole business."

"I'm sorry."

"It's okay, forget it."

He grinned. "I'm Matt Zaharis."

"Greek?"

"Once upon a time, back a couple of generations."

She put out her hand. "I'm Andrea Stafford."

"That's right. That old man in the car yesterday called you Andy. I noticed that." He took her hand and she shook his firmly. Her skin was cool and dry. He was conscious that his own hand was sweaty. "Wet hands are a sign of character," he told her quickly.

She laughed. "Good or bad?"

He shrugged. "Is Andy your nickname?"

She nodded. "That old man in the car yesterday was my father. He's always called me Andy."

Matt winced. "Sorry, I didn't mean to . . ."

"Well, he *is* old," she said, coming to his rescue.

"He looked familiar, like I'd seen him before."

"He's Stark Stafford, the poet."

"Son of a gun!" Matt flushed when he realized how foolish he sounded. "Sure, 'A Winter's Eve.' I memorized part of that poem for a Christmas program at school a couple years ago."

She laughed. "God, I'd better not tell Daddy that. He would hate to know he was being force-fed to school kids."

Her reference to kids bothered him. "Well, I'm much older now, and I still like the poem."

"That's good." She giggled, then forced a straight face. "I'm glad you like his work."

"What's so funny?"

"Nothing, really." She looked away. "I've got to go. My father will be wanting lunch." She started off along the bluff above the lake.

"Wait a second," he shouted. He ran to catch up with her. "Mind if I walk part of the way with you? I still might spot something interesting today."

She looked at him out of the corners of her eyes.

"Birds, I mean," he added, tapping his field glasses.

Andrea was wearing cutoffs and a white blouse, the sleeves rolled up. When she walked ahead of him on the path above the rocks, he couldn't help noticing that although her figure was full, she was not fat. Pleasingly plump, as his mother frequently referred to his fat Aunt Kate, only in Andrea's case it was true.

He was glad of the distraction when a flock of large birds flew out of a clump of pines, their wings whistling as they beat away into the barrens.

"What was that?" Andrea asked, stopping to watch them disappear.

"Mourning doves," he told her. "You've probably heard them if you've been walking around here. They have a long, low call. It sounds sad."

"We only just bought our cottage from a friend. I haven't been out here much."

"Where are you from?"

"Boston."

They followed the path into a large, overgrown field. At the lakeside a boathouse perched on the edge of the water. At the top of the field a large summer house sprawled along the hillside, all gray-weathered shingles and squares of glass.

"Cottage?" Matt said.

"Well, yeah. It's not winterized."

"Around here we call places like that . . ." He hesitated. "Well, we don't call them cottages."

They stopped near the boathouse. One end was in the water; it creaked in movement to the small waves that the wind drove across the lake. Far off in the distance a bell was ringing, softly but persistently.

"That's Daddy's bell," Andrea said. "I have to go."

He wanted to ask her why her father had to ring a bell for her, but he didn't get the chance. She was already running up the field toward the house.

"I'll see you," he called.

She stopped halfway to the top to wave at him. Then she ran on, through the tall, unmowed meadow grass, over the edge of the hill and out of sight. He lingered for a while near the woods, pretending to be watching for birds coming into the field, but she did not appear again.

That night in his room while noting down his bird observations, he wanted to add something about his encounter with Andrea. But he didn't see how it would fit into a scientific journal.

# Chapter 5

*M*att searched every acre of the pine barrens during the next few days, looking for the multicolored bird. He didn't see it again, nor did he see Andrea Stafford again either, although he didn't realize at first that he was watching for her, too.

In his journal he wrote:

> *July 17*
> *The loons are gone from the lake. I haven't seen a single one all summer. I wonder if they're gone for good. Is it because of all the boats around the islands where they used to nest?*

And the next day:

> *July 18*
> *Spent all morning looking for that strange bird I saw on the 14th. I'm beginning to think I imagined it. But maybe it*

*was an escaped pet bird. Maybe something
has already killed it.*

He wanted to go up on Firetop Mountain and see if
he could find the ravens. It was something he did each
year, a kind of pilgrimage, his way of remembering the
time when he got lost on the mountain.

He hadn't been up on Firetop all summer. But he
didn't go up there now. He continued to patrol the pine
barrens.

He added to the bottom of one journal entry:

> *Sometimes I think birds are like feelings
> with wings, a lot of different feelings, rising
> and falling. And free, not locked up inside
> somewhere.*

And then he crossed this out because he didn't think it
belonged in a scientific journal either.

After a week he crossed the barrens one morning to the
field below Andrea Stafford's house. He stood at the edge
of the grass and looked up at the house. It was then he
realized that he had been hoping he would run into her
again.

The thought frightened him so much he started to turn
back into the woods. She and her father had probably
gone back to Boston, their vacation over. If he went up
over the hill to the house and knocked on the door, no
one would answer.

He walked along the path into the woods, then stopped,
reversed his direction once more, and walked toward the

boathouse at the water's edge. He'd see if it would make a good place to use as a blind in the fall when the large flocks of ducks stopped on the lake on their way south.

One side of the boathouse had been converted to a screened porch; the screens sagged in the middle, sported patches wherever they had rusted through. As he stepped carefully onto the deck that ran beside the porch, he saw movement through the screens.

"You startled me."

He walked closer and peered in. Andrea was sitting at a picnic table, a sketch pad before her, a pencil in her hand.

"You really gave me a start," she said again.

"Sorry." He looked around for the door.

"Out bird watching?"

He nodded.

"See anything interesting?"

"Saw a powerboat just miss Barrel Rock out there. I don't think the turkey at the wheel even knew it was there. Too bad he missed."

"Oh, bloodthirsty." She smiled at him.

He shrugged. "The summer people make me sick, roaring up and down the lake like they own it, like no one else has any right to . . ." He found the door and stepped inside. She quickly closed her sketch pad.

"You really hate them," she said.

"We had several loons that used to nest out on the islands. But the boats bothered them so much, they're gone now."

"Maybe it was something else."

He realized he was beginning to sound like a crank, like Old Man Smitty, the janitor at school, who thought the world had gone completely into the hands of the devil twenty years ago, and he was just hanging on to see if anyone else would notice. He grinned. "Don't mind me."

"I don't."

They stared at each other. "What are you drawing?" he asked.

"Oh, nothing really." She put down her pencil, then picked it up again. "Nothing."

"Let's see."

"No, I'm really no good."

"I bet you're great. I bet you draw as well as your father writes poems."

She shook her head. "No way."

"Come on. I'm the art critic for the *Ellington News*. I could be useful in your career."

"No, Matthew, I don't want to show them to you."

Why didn't he stop before he made a complete idiot out of himself? He lunged for the pad.

"Matthew!"

"It's Matt."

She snatched the pad off the table and retreated to the far end of the porch. Instead of letting her go, he chased her and pulled the pad out of her hands. He climbed onto the picnic table where she couldn't reach him and opened the pad.

"Give it back, Matt."

"Not till I see what you're hiding. Let's check it out." He opened the pad and looked at the first drawing. "A

nice little sketch of the famous Lake Craddock Islands."
He held it up as if he were displaying it for an audience,
ignoring Andrea's attempts to take back the pad.

"Then we have, ah yes, a nifty little study of a mourning dove." Again he held up the drawing for the imag-
inary audience.

"You're an ass," Andrea told him.

"No, no, an art critic." He turned to the last drawing. "Hey, that's us, walking in the barrens the other
day." He stared at the likeness of himself walking beside
her in the drawing. It was as if she had found some way
to be in two places at one time, to walk there beside him
and yet follow behind, sketch pad in hand, drawing the
two of them totally unaware.

"It's good, it's really good," he said, stepping down off
the table. "How did you do this one?"

She grabbed the pad out of his hands. Her face was
red. "I just did it."

He knew he had gone too far, but apologizing now
would only make things worse.

As if reading his mind, she said, "Do you always act
so crazy?"

He shook his head. "No, I don't. I really don't."

"Sure."

The tension between them was so thick it seemed to
blot out the sunlight coming through the screens, isolat-
ing them on the porch.

"What can I say?" he mumbled at last.

"Don't say anything." A bell began to ring at the house
up on the hill. The wind off the lake blew the sound of

the bell away once, then blew it away again. But it kept coming back.

"That's my father." Andrea gathered up her drawing pencils. "I'd better go up."

"Why does he ring for you that way?" Matt asked.

"He's blind," she said. At the door that led out onto the deck, she paused. "Look, I usually have my mornings free, while he's writing. I'm usually down here, or up in the garden near the house."

He followed her onto the deck, where she stopped again. "Oh, screw it," she said. "Why don't you come to dinner tonight?"

Startled by her sudden vehemence, he could only nod.

"Can you come, around eight?"

"Sure."

"Do you know the way by the road?"

"Yes." He looked up at the house. The bell was ringing steadily now. "I'll recognize the house from the road."

"If you don't there's a signboard nailed to a tree by the drive. Gunfire. You can't miss it."

"Why is it called Gunfire?"

She shrugged. "I have no idea." Ten feet out into the field she turned to look at him again. "Your parents won't mind your coming, will they?"

He shook his head impatiently. "I'm on my own this summer."

"Oh. Then we'll see you around eight."

He watched her go. Her long skirt billowed out, dragging behind her as if to hold her back, as if to catch her fast there among the tall yellow spears of grass.

\*       \*       \*

In the evening Matt went upstairs to take a shower and put on a clean pair of jeans and his denim jacket, leaving John in the kitchen wolfing down a supper of canned chili. Matt hoped to sneak out the front door unnoticed, but John was lurking near the foot of the stairs when he came down.

"Well, look at you, all slicked up for a night on the town. Who's the lucky lady?"

"No one you know."

John laughed. He was working on a beer. "Come on, who is it?"

"I'm having dinner with the Staffords."

"Who are they?"

"Stark Stafford is the poet. His daughter was driving the Mercedes last week, the one you wouldn't back up for."

John raised his beer can in a mock toast. "Well, moving up in the world. Going over to the enemy camp."

Matt shrugged.

"Got time for a beer?"

Matt glanced at the clock on the mantelpiece. "Not really."

"Come on, I'll drive you over if you want. You got time."

Matt began straightening up the living room while John went after the beer. When John came back, Matt continued to pick up the litter on the floor.

"Leave that, I'll get it later." John opened the can of beer and handed it to him.

"This place has been a disaster area ever since Mom and Dad left," Matt said, taking the beer. "We got to try, at least. Got to keep up appearances."

"Why?"

"Suppose Mrs. Gannon comes over." Matt waved one hand at the room. "Suppose she sees this? Suppose Mom calls her to check up on us and finds out we're living like pigs?"

"If you're so worried about it, feel free." John sank down onto the couch. "So tell me about your girl friend."

"She's not my girl friend."

"Well, when do I get to meet her?"

Matt sipped his beer. His stomach was so tense the beer immediately came back up. He swallowed hard. "Don't hold your breath."

For a moment John looked hurt and Matt regretted his sharp reply. There was always this hostility between them, this habit of putting each other down, even when they were pretending to have a friendly conversation.

John drained his beer and crushed the can in his hand. "Is she that ugly? I didn't get much of a look at her the other day."

Matt shook his head. "She's not ugly." Was it just that they didn't know any other way to act toward each other, no way except to quarrel, exchange insults, make jokes at each other's expense? Or was there something more? He took a last sip of his beer and put the can down on the coffee table.

"I have to get going."

John started to stand up, but Matt waved for him to stay put. "I'll ride over on my bike."

"Suit yourself."

On the front porch Matt stopped and looked back.

"I'm going to clean up this whole damn house tomorrow."

"Whatever turns you on."

Matt tried to swallow his anger with the beer that didn't want to stay down. "Don't you think it matters, John?" he demanded. "Don't you think it matters that Mom and Dad shouldn't have to worry about us while they're away?"

"You tell me."

Matt gave up. As he wheeled his bike from the garage, John came out on the side steps, another beer in his hand.

"Shall I wait up?" he asked in a falsetto voice.

Matt didn't reply. He pedaled quickly up the street, reaching the corner before the beer in his stomach decided it was coming back up for good.

# Chapter 6

*T*he summer people were enjoying steaks tonight. Matt could smell each barbecue as he pedaled along the south side of the lake. The water was a flat, pale blue, except where one fleeing motorboat plowed the surface far out among the splashes of orange and red reflected from the setting sun. The rocky dome of Firetop Mountain in the northwest beyond the lake still glowed with a warm yellow light, but the valleys below it, facing east, were already in blue and purple shadow.

He did not pedal hard, not wanting to arrive at the Staffords' house in a sweat. He lingered in the shadows under the trees, where the air was cool and damp, then walked his bike up two of the steeper hills. He was torn between his fear of being late and his fear of getting there.

In front of many of the cottages, orange outdoor lights were already burning in the early dusk. They stretched before him like a string of party decorations. From the hillside on his left, music drifted down from a large dance hall; close by, a screen door slammed, a baby cried.

He did not ride into the dark pine barrens, but continued along the paved street to Westerly Road, where he turned north around the far side of the barrens. Here, in the gloom below the ridge, he swerved onto the shoulder of the road to avoid a speeding sports car.

When he got to the Staffords' house there were lights on for him, and he could plainly see the sign announcing that this was Gunfire. He swung into the drive and pedaled over the gravel to the front steps. Andrea was standing just inside the doorway.

"Right on time," she said. She held the screen door open for him. In the dimly lighted front hall, her arm brushed against his. She was wearing a summer dress with a stone pendant at her throat. He was glad now that he had put on his denim jacket.

"Come inside. Are you hungry?"

"Yes," he lied.

A long table in the dining room was decorated with candles. There were only two places set.

"We're having white wine with the meal," Andrea told him. "Would you like a glass now?"

He nodded. He stifled an impulse to wipe his sweaty hands on his jeans. "That would be nice."

She went into the kitchen after the wine. While she was gone, he stood beside the table. Should he sit down? Which place was his? Where was her father?

"Sit on the far side," Andrea told him, as if she had guessed his dilemma. "That will put me closer to the kitchen." She placed the bottle of wine on the table and handed him the corkscrew. "But first open this, please."

As he struggled with the cork, she stood there watching him. He began to think it was a test. He got the corkscrew in at last, but it was too far to the side and the cork crumbled when he tried to pull it out.

"Nasty little devil," Andrea said. "If we have to, we'll smash the neck off on the edge of the table and drink like pirates."

He tried again. Somewhere beyond them in the dark house, out of reach of the candlelight, a clock struck eight.

"Daddy's not feeling up to joining us tonight," Andrea said, as if the striking clock had told her so. She picked up a fork and put it down again. "I didn't think he would."

Dinner was fresh salad with a light oil and vinegar dressing, rock cornish game hens (one for each of them), hot biscuits, peas cooked with small onions, early potatoes that had been roasted whole with the game hens. They were halfway through the meal before Matt realized Andrea was doing everything herself. He had imagined that there would be maids and cooks in a house like this.

He offered to help when she went after more biscuits.

"No, stay there. I don't like people in my kitchen."

He watched her walk away from the table. Again he was confused about how old she was. Her remark about her kitchen was something his mother might have said.

When she came back with the biscuits, she poured them both more wine. He tried to look away as she leaned across the table to fill his glass.

She laughed. "This dress makes me look like a cow."

"No, it . . ." He felt his face grow warm. "It's a nice dress."

Their eyes met for a second as she settled back in her chair. "You like the word *nice*. You've used it four times since you got here."

"Have I?"

She nodded. She buttered half a biscuit and slipped it into her mouth.

"Well, it's a good word," he said, trying to sound sure of himself. "Useful."

She shook her head. "It's a dreadful word. People hide behind it. If you want to look down the front of my dress, do it. Don't tell me my dress is *nice*."

He picked up one of the little drumsticks from his game hen and nibbled off the last of the meat.

"Is the hen nice?" she asked.

He shook his head. "No, it's . . ." He looked at her eyes. "It's different. I like it."

She smiled. "That's better. You're a fast learner." She reached for her wine. The light from the candles reflected off the glass. "A toast," she said.

He picked up his own glass.

"To never being nice."

They drank.

"Now finish up," she said. "I've made us a perfectly wicked dessert."

Over coffee and strawberry pie she said, "Are you really an admirer of my father's poetry?"

He nodded. She was looking at him as if she expected something more. "I like it," he said.

53

"What do you like?"

"'A Winter's Eve,' especially the part I memorized." He searched his memory. "'Lost in snowdrifts of my seasons past, so terribly white, so colorless at last.'"

She clapped her hands. "Very good! Have you seen his last book?"

He shook his head.

Andrea got up and disappeared into a room at the front of the house. When she turned on a light, its yellow glow spilled out over the hardwood floor. She was leafing through a book as she came back.

"It's signed," she told him. "You'll have to tell us what you think when you've had time to read it." She handed him the book.

He glanced at the cover: *Sound Side*. The name Stark Stafford appeared on the spine, larger than the title. "May I keep it?"

She laughed. "That's why I gave it to you." She began gathering up the dishes. "More coffee?"

"No, I'm . . ."

She was already taking the larger plates and serving bowls into the kitchen. By the time she came back, he had the rest of the dishes piled in neat stacks. Despite her protests he followed her into the kitchen and dried while she washed. The overhead light hummed faintly.

"I've got to help," he told her. "Wouldn't be right to leave it all for you."

"Your mother's got you well trained," she said.

He shrugged, pretending her words had not carried any sting. Through the window over the sink he could

see, beyond the reflections of themselves, the lights out-
lining Point Rollins.

"Is your father ill?" he asked.

Andrea seemed to hesitate before answering. "He's been
under a strain lately," she said at last. She squirted more
detergent into the water. "His next book of poems is due
out this winter and he still hasn't written the major
piece for it, the keystone poem he needs to pull the others
together. He's been working on some articles for *The
New Yorker* instead."

He helped her put the dishes away. The kitchen was
enormous, the cupboards high along the far wall, near
the door leading into the spicy smells of the pantry.

"Are you here alone?" he asked as she handed him
the last platter.

She nodded. "It's just Daddy and me," she said proudly,
as if she were bragging. "He doesn't like having strangers
around. Otherwise we'd have at least a cook. Money's
no problem. It's never been a problem. There's always
been money . . ."

Her voice trailed off as she untied her apron. She shook
her hair from the back of her neck. "Daddy inherited his
father's fertilizer fortune." She suddenly laughed. "He
doesn't like that to be common knowledge."

"So you do everything?" he asked as they walked back
into the dining room.

"It's not that much, really. And I have my mornings
free while he's writing." She looked at him. "It's a good
life. We've traveled all over the world."

"What about school?"

"I've had tutors mostly." She pulled the cloth from the table, and they folded it together.

"Tutors?"

"Sure." She took the folded cloth and placed it on top of a high sideboard. Her face appeared in the mirror. He thought it must be a trick of the glass, to make her look so angry. "They've given me a better education than any I could have gotten in schools."

He didn't argue with her, but she went on anyway. "Daddy's writing is important. I have to make allowances for it, try to fit other things around it."

She turned toward him. "I know what you're thinking."

"How do you know what I'm thinking?"

"I do. You're thinking I'm getting the short end of the stick. Well, last winter I spent December and half of January in Paris. Where were *you* last winter?"

He grinned. "Kicking my way through three feet of snow right here in good old Bredstone."

"And I had a lover who was an official in the French government. What did you do for excitement last winter?"

He tried to hide his surprise at how freely she spoke of her private life. "Oh me? I flunked German, and over Christmas my brother John and I had a snowball fight up on Oak Hill and he broke one of my front teeth."

She wasn't smiling. "After Paris we spent two weeks in Monaco," she said. "I won five hundred dollars at the roulette tables."

"Okay."

"So don't waste your time feeling sorry for me."

"I won't."

"I have a good life."

"Sounds like you do." He looked around at the door leading into the front hall. "It's late. I'd better go."

"I thought you told me you're on your own this summer."

"I did. I mean, I am."

"Then why do you have to leave now?"

He shrugged. "I guess I don't have to leave."

In the living room she turned on a second light. One wall of the room was taken up by a high stone fireplace, now cold, swept clean. Andrea sank down in the middle of the couch and watched him wander around the room.

"Put on some music," she said, nodding toward the stereo in one corner.

He began flipping through the pile of records on the shelf. "What do you want to hear?"

"Put on some Mozart. But keep it low so my father won't hear." He held up one album and she nodded. "I hope he's asleep," she said softly, as if to herself.

"Is Stark your father's real name?" he asked her. He was sitting in a large, overstuffed chair that matched the couch.

She shook her head. "It's a nickname from college. His real name is Theodore, and he hates it. That was his father's name, too."

Around them the music formed a soft cushion of sound, filling the room from the speakers at each end of one long wall.

"Do you like classical music?" she asked.

He shrugged. "I haven't heard enough of it to know."

"Two years ago we went to a music festival in Vienna. My mother even showed up for a few days, and all three of us . . ."

"Are your parents divorced?" he interrupted. He was growing tired of her bragging about all the places she'd been.

"Have been for years. Mom couldn't take . . ." she stopped.

While he waited for her to go on, the record came to the end of the first side. He got up and flipped it over.

"How old are you, Matt?" she asked while his back was turned.

"Almost sixteen."

He felt as if she were setting up a competition between them. "How old are you?" he asked. "Sometimes you look twenty, other times you could be my age."

"Somewhere in there, between the two," she said with a smile.

"You aren't going to narrow it down for me?"

She shook her head. "If you ever figure it out, I'll tell you if you're right."

"Eighteen."

Again she shook her head. "Would you like a drink?"

"Maybe if there's some wine left."

When she came back, she was carrying two large glasses, an inch of amber fluid in each. "The wine is all gone. This is brandy." She handed him his glass, then sat on the arm of his chair. One fold of her dress touched his knee. He took a drink of his brandy, then started to choke.

58

She laughed. "Just sip it."

"I am."

"How come you're on your own this summer?"

"My parents are in Europe." He felt a certain amount of satisfaction in being able to tell her this.

"And they left you here all alone?"

"No, my brother's here too. He's three years older than me."

"That's right, your stubborn brother who hates to back up." She laughed. "What's he like when he isn't being stubborn?"

Matt felt a stab of jealousy, as if she might be thinking that she would find someone John's age more interesting. "He's a turkey," he said.

She laughed. "Really?"

"Really. Biggest turkey I've ever known."

"What's he think about you?"

"Thinks I'm the biggest turkey he's ever known."

"Well, that works out conveniently, doesn't it?"

Again he had the impression she was older than she looked. He sipped his brandy, being more careful this time. When the turntable shut itself off, she got up to put on another record. While she was looking through the albums, a loud shout came from upstairs.

She whirled around and looked toward the stairs. All composure was suddenly gone from her face.

"What was that?" Matt asked, halfway out of his chair.

"Andy! Andy!" The shouting ended in a groan.

"You'd better go," Andrea told him as she headed for the stairs.

When he hesitated by the dining room doorway, she

hurried him on. "Please. You can find your own way out, can't you?"

Something heavy fell upstairs.

"Do you need some help?" Matt asked her.

She shook her head and started up the stairs. "Meet me at the boathouse tomorrow," she said, and then she was gone.

# Chapter 7

*M*att waited at the boathouse all morning. He glanced often up the hill toward the gray-shingled house to see if Andrea had come out onto the hillside. Disappointed each time, he would then look to the left, training his field glasses on the edge of the woods. All morning he heard a mourning dove calling nearby, but he could not find it with his glasses.

Behind him the lake waves splashed against the edge of the boathouse. He sat on the deck, his back to the water. Overhead, dull gray clouds screened out the sun. A few raindrops splattered onto the deck. If it began to rain hard, he would leave.

Last night the sound of the shouting at Andrea's house had followed him home. Even the lights near the town beach did not drive the chill from his spine.

As he lay in bed reading late into the night, he kept recalling the look on Andrea's face as she asked him to leave. One moment she seemed so sure of herself, making him believe she was too old for him, too sophisticated, making him feel that their budding friendship was a joke, something he had concocted all by himself, in his own mind only. Then the shouting upstairs broke the spell, and her confidence fell apart.

He wanted to ask her why, if she ever came down from the house.

A steady rain began to fall. It tapped on the deck, whispered on the lake behind him. He took shelter inside the screened porch. He had no real idea what time it was, but he knew he had been waiting for hours.

When the rain let up briefly, he abandoned the boathouse and headed toward the barrens, where he had left his bike in a grove of poplars. Angry at himself for waiting so long, for worrying about Andrea when he hardly knew her, he refused to look even one more time up the hill to the house. He was at the edge of the woods when he heard someone call his name.

Turning around, he saw her running down from the house. For a second he thought of pretending he had not seen her. He might just slip away into the barrens, as if he did not know she was running breakneck through the tall grass toward him. It would serve her right for keeping him waiting there all morning, for making him worry about her as if he gave a damn what . . .

He stopped, ashamed of his sudden mean feelings. He walked back into the field to meet her.

"Matt," she said. Her jeans were soaked to the knees from her run through the wet grass.

He nodded.

"You're angry, I know. Have you been waiting long?"

"A while."

"I tried to get down sooner. Didn't you hear me calling you? I thought you were ignoring me."

He did not admit that he had tried. He hunched his shoulders as the rain began to fall again. "We're getting wet," he said, as if she might not have noticed.

"Come on." She grabbed his hand and they ran toward the boathouse. Inside the porch she shook the rain out of her hair. When she looked over at him, her eyes were hidden behind the wet, dark strands that had fallen across her face.

"About last night," she said.

He waited. Above them from the house the bell began to ring.

She made a face.

"You just got here," he said.

"I know. He can be difficult when the writing isn't going well." She pulled her hair out of her eyes. "I'm sorry I had to run out on you last night."

He shrugged.

"Daddy has these dreams that he can see again. He gets up in his sleep and walks into things, and then he wakes up and he can't see and . . ." She looked away, out over the lake. "The dreams bring back all the horror, all the fear." She looked back at him. "You can understand that, can't you?"

He nodded. "Yes, I can."

She studied his face, as if searching for some sign that he was lying to her. The bell continued to ring from the house. Even the rain on the boathouse roof could not drown it out.

"You're sure?" she asked at last.

"Sure." He grinned. "I'm sure."

"Now I'm going to have to leave, and I just got here and you've been waiting all morning."

He shrugged as if it did not matter. His anger was gone.

"Look, Matt," she said, pausing at the door beside the deck. "If it stops raining, Daddy wants to go to the Audenville Fair tonight. He needs material for one of the articles he's writing. Would you like to drive over with us?"

Was it only his imagination, or did she sound as if she wanted very much for him to say yes, he would go?

"I'd like to."

She smiled for the first time that morning. "We can pick you up in town."

"Okay. In front of Antonio's Market."

"Around seven. We'll grab something to eat there. Daddy wants to experience the whole milieu."

"The whole what?"

She laughed. "The whole thing about being at a small-town New England fair."

"Oh. Sure. Maybe we can go on a few of the rides. I threw up once on the Dragonflier." He wondered why he didn't shut up.

Her laughter followed her out into the rain. He watched her run back across the field, staying by the boathouse until the bell finally stopped ringing.

When Andrea parked the black Mercedes in front of Antonio's Market at ten minutes past seven, she was alone.

"Where's your father?" he asked as he climbed into the front beside her.

She didn't answer, handing him, instead, the signed copy of *Sound Side* he had forgotten to take home with him. "Here, you left this behind last night."

"Sorry."

"No problem."

As they drove out of town he glanced at her several times. She was wearing a yellow rain slicker even though the rain had stopped two hours ago. He was secretly glad her father was again absent.

"Daddy asked me to do his local color for him," she said after a while. A few drops of rain came down off a tree and splattered on the windshield. She turned on the wipers.

"Local color?"

She frowned. "You know, bits and pieces to make his article fresh and authentic."

"And you can do that for him?"

"Sure. I act as his eyes all the time."

They drove north along the east side of the lake. The motels they passed already had their signs flashing under the gloomy, overcast sky. As they approached Audenville in its valley north of the lake, tatters of gray cloud drifted across the hills surrounding the town. The lights of the fairgrounds glowed in the distance like small, colorless candles.

"There's a college up here, isn't there?" Andrea asked.

He nodded. "Yeah. Audenville State. It's a branch of the state university."

"Is that where you'll go?"

He shrugged. "I don't know yet." He sensed that she was just making conversation. "I'm glad you came without your father," he told her.

She looked away from her driving. Her face was white.

"I mean, I'm glad you decided to come even though he decided not to."

She nodded.

He wondered what it would take to get her to smile. For once he was fresh out of jokes.

The fair had been set up on three large fields east of the center of town. Andrea ignored his outstretched hand and paid the admission charge for both of them. As they rolled into the crowded parking lot, she told him to put away his money.

"Then I'll buy supper," he insisted.

"All right," she said.

They ate hot dogs at a stand at the edge of the midway, then bought fried dough a few feet further on. Before they reached the rides, they had worked their way through cotton candy, caramel apples, and two ice cream sundaes. Andrea took only a bite or two of each food, then threw it way. She had a notebook in the pocket of her slicker, and each time she ate something, she jotted down a line or two.

He ignored this for as long as he could. Then he took the sundae she was about to throw into a trash can and gave it to a small boy walking by. "Haven't you ever been to a carnival before?"

She shook her head. She walked up to a booth where

a large woman in a red plastic coat was dishing out spareribs.

"Do you travel with the carnival, or are you a local?"

The woman looked at her. "You want to buy something, or what?"

Andrea bought a plate of spareribs and handed it to Matt without eating any. "What's it like traveling from town to town?"

The spareribs were hot and greasy. Matt had lost his appetite. He watched with embarrassment as Andrea continued to bombard the woman in the red plastic coat with questions. All she got back as answers were noncommittal grunts.

"Imbecile!" Andrea said as they walked away. She took out her notebook and wrote something down with a slash of her pen.

Matt extended the plate of spareribs. "Want some?"

Andrea looked down at the paper plate. "Oh God, Matt. Throw it *away*."

"You just spent three dollars for it."

"So what? I'm certainly not going to eat that greasy filth."

He looked around in vain for another hungry kid, then found a trash barrel and dropped the plate of spareribs on top of a pile of soda cans. "Well, what do you want to do next?" he asked as brightly as he could.

"Let's go check out the rides."

But it soon became apparent that Andrea wasn't interested in *riding* on the rides. With Matt trailing behind, she cornered various men working the machinery and asked them about their work, their lives, their plans for the future. She had better luck with the men; they all took an interest in her.

Matt watched her fill up the pages of her notebook with the more colorful things they told her. The suggestions from some of the men that she come with them to their trailers at the edge of the fairgrounds for more details did not even make her pause in her writing. It was as if she didn't hear these suggestions, didn't see the expressions on the men's faces when they made them.

On the walk from the airplane ride to the Ferris wheel, he touched her arm to get her attention. She looked up from the page she was filling with neat little sentences and brushed back her hair.

"What is it, Matt?"

"It's not really so cool, talking to all these guys the way you are."

She laughed. The crowd swept past them along the midway. "Why shouldn't I talk to them?"

He looked back over his shoulder, toward the last man she had questioned, who was still watching them. "They're . . ."

She shook her head impatiently. "Oh, stop being such a wimp. They're roustabouts. They're supposed to act rough."

Stung, he looked down at her notebook. "I'm serious. Don't you hear what they're saying to you?"

"Sure, I'm writing down almost everything."

"But they keep leering at you."

"Don't you ever look at girls? Seems to me I remember

you last night looking down the front of my dress every chance you got."

He shook his head, forcing himself to look directly at her. "That's different."

She laughed.

"Let's go on the Ferris wheel. You've got enough notes."

"Go on if you want. I'm not done yet."

She walked over to the Ferris wheel and found one of the roustabouts lounging against a low fence, watching the crowd. When she started talking to him, he stood up straight.

"You a reporter?" he asked.

She nodded. "Sort of."

"I'm on my break now." He pointed toward an area marked off with colored nylon rope. Inside the rough rectangle, there were a dozen white tables. Over a small booth to one side a tattered plastic banner rattled in the wind, fluttering with pictures of wine bottles and beer cans and the words BEER GARDEN in large, crude letters.

"Buy me a drink and I'll tell you anything you want to know, honey," the roustabout said.

"Andrea?"

She turned toward Matt and impatiently waved him away. "Go enjoy yourself. I'll meet you later at the car."

Matt watched her go into the beer garden with the man. He called to her again, but she ignored him. She had her hands thrust deep into the pockets of her rain slicker, holding on to her notebook and her pen. When the roustabout touched her back, she stepped to one side, away from him, but she kept right on walking toward the table he had picked out.

If Matt had come on his bike, he would have left her there and gone home, but he did not relish the long walk back to Bredstone. He bought himself a ticket on the Ferris wheel and climbed into one of the cars. He was jerked slowly upward as the attendant filled the cars below him.

At the top he looked toward the southwest. He could see a curtain of mist rising over the distant lake. In all the darkness of the hills beyond the lights of Audenville the lake mist was the only thing that wasn't dark.

Matt rode on the Ferris wheel twice. He gazed down at the lights and the people below, at the arena at the far edge of the fairgrounds, at the pens for livestock beyond. As he swung down each time through the far side of his arc, he could see Andrea sitting at the table in the beer garden, talking with the same roustabout. Once when he passed over he saw her walking away, back toward the midway. As he began to climb again, he saw the man get up and follow her.

He craned his neck to keep track of them as the Ferris wheel continued to climb. Andrea's yellow rain slicker disappeared into the crowd; a moment later the roustabout disappeared too, right behind her.

He had to wait for the ride to finish. It seemed to go on forever. He stared down into the crowds below him the whole time, trying to spot Andrea again, hoping he would see her come toward the Ferris wheel.

But she didn't.

By the time he got back onto the ground he was sweating, even though the night was cool and damp. He ran to the midway and searched for her there, then searched the darker paths behind the booths on either side. As he pushed through the groups of people crowded around the games of chance, clustered about the stands selling popcorn, hot dogs, barbecued chicken, wedges of apple pie, he had to bite his lip to keep from shouting her name.

Giving up on the midway, he walked into the shadowy area beside the arena, near the path from the parking lot they had used earlier. Maybe she had gone back to the car to wait for him there.

The crowd was thin near the arena, which was closed for the night. In one of the dark portals Matt spotted a movement up against the closed steel gate. He looked again. Something yellow . . .

He ran toward the gate. The roustabout had Andrea backed up against the steel bars. He was pulling at her slicker. "I've got to go back to the car," Andrea was telling him. She kept saying it over and over again as she tried to pull away from him, as if she thought it was a magic incantation that had to be said three times, seven times, twelve times before it would work. "I've got to go back to the car . . ."

When Andrea saw Matt running toward them, she tried to dart under the man's arms. He grabbed the sleeve of her coat and slammed her back against the gate.

"Leave her alone." The words all came out in a rush, and they were only a whisper. Matt tried again, his legs shaking so hard he thought he would fall over. "Leave her alone."

71

"Look who's here," the roustabout said as he turned around. "Get lost, kid." His voice was harsh, like an animal's growl.

Then Andrea yelled so loud the arena echoed behind her. She kicked out with one foot and the man stepped back, out of range. Matt dashed forward, grabbed Andrea's arm, and began pulling her toward the parking lot. Enraged, the roustabout lunged after them, knocking them to the ground. Matt got up, found Andrea's hand again, pulled her up onto her feet.

They reached the path. Several cars were driving out of the parking lot together, their headlights shining through the dust. Andrea ran toward them. Matt was close behind. When he looked back, the roustabout had disappeared into the shadows.

When they found the Mercedes, Andrea let herself in and locked her door. He had to tap on the glass. She leaned across and unlocked the door on his side.

"Sorry," she said.

He climbed into the front.

"Lock your door," she said.

"He's gone now."

"I don't care. Lock your door."

Her voice was as thin and tight as the twang of a rubber band stretched to its breaking point. He locked the door.

"Want me to drive?" he asked. He was still shaking all over. He hoped that in the darkness inside the car she wouldn't notice.

She ignored his offer, starting the car herself and driving slowly out of the parking lot. Matt thought she was doing fine until he realized she was paying no attention to the traffic cop trying to stop her with his flashlight.

"Andrea!"

She slammed on the brakes. The traffic cop yelled something at her.

"Maybe we should tell him what happened," Matt suggested.

"No."

When the traffic cop signaled for her to pull ahead, she floored the gas and spun out onto the road, sending back a shower of dirt and stones. Matt looked back and saw the traffic cop waving his flashlight, screaming at them. He faced forward again just in time to see that Andrea had skidded into the wrong lane.

"Let me drive."

"No, I'm all right." She slowed down, steering the car over to the right. "I'm all right now."

They drove home in silence. He wanted to ask her how someone so sophisticated could do something so dumb, but he realized it would sound too much like saying I told you so, so he didn't. As they came into town he said, "You can drop me off anywhere."

She parked a block down from Antonio's Market. Before Matt could climb out of the car, she picked up the copy of *Sound Side* from the seat and pushed it into his hands.

"Don't forget this again," she whispered.

He took it from her and opened the door on his side. Suddenly her hand was on his arm. "Thank you."

"All I did was distract him by letting him knock me down." He thought it was a pretty good joke, considering the circumstances.

She didn't laugh. Instead, she leaned over and kissed him.

"Good-night, Matt."

He climbed out, then stood there watching Andrea drive through a red light on her way back to the lake.

He walked home the long way, and when he discovered that John was having another party, he quickly escaped through a vacant lot and wandered onto the quiet streets in the Oak Hill section of town. He couldn't go home right now, not to any party, not to John, not to anyone.

When the town police car suddenly appeared at the far corner of the street, Matt ducked behind a hedge. He watched August Burns drive slowly by. He felt like a criminal, hiding there in the shadows, but he did not come out until the police car was gone.

# Chapter 8

John had left him a note taped to the refrigerator door. Matt found it the next morning when he was getting milk for his cereal.

> *Matt,*
> *Mom called last night. That's twice you haven't been here when she's called and I'm getting tired of thinking up excuses for you. She said she's going to call again this morning, our time, so make damn sure you're here.*
>
> *John*

He read it twice, then crumpled it up and threw it toward the already-overflowing wastebasket beside the sink.

The house smelled of stale beer and cigarette smoke. He cleared himself a spot at the table and ate his cereal without tasting it. John was sound asleep in his room, probably wouldn't be awake for hours.

The house was peaceful despite the mess left from

John's party last night. Matt sat for a long time over a cup of coffee, not reading, not tempted by the television in the side room. He listened to sounds from outside: cars driving by the house, a garbage truck loading over on Broderick Court, a persistent robin in the lilac bushes beside the garage. He was glad John was still sleeping, he was glad he was alone.

His life seemed to have turned itself upside down in the past couple of days. And the proof of this was that even as he enjoyed this quiet time alone, he was impatient to be off again. As soon as he had talked with his mother, he would ride over to the barrens and walk to the boathouse.

Andrea would be there. He was pretty sure of that.

While he waited for his mother's call, he gathered up all the dirty clothes he could find and jammed them into the washing machine along with a cup of detergent. They were in the dryer when the telephone finally rang. As he ran for it, he tripped over some cushions John's friends had left on the floor.

"Matt?"

He was surprised that his mother's voice sounded so clear, as if she were calling from a booth downtown.

"Hi, Mom."

"Well, it's a relief to know you're still alive."

"Sure I'm alive."

She paused for a moment before she went on. "John assured us you were just fine, but a mother likes to know these things firsthand."

"I'm fine."

"You're eating well-balanced meals?"

"Sure. Where are you calling from?"

"Paris."

"Is it nice?" He heard what he had said and quickly added, "Is it exciting?"

"It's very nice, dear." His mother wasn't going to be distracted from her main concerns. "How are you and your brother getting along?"

It would have been easiest to say everything in that department was just fine, couldn't be better, but his mother would know *that* was a lie. "Okay, I guess," Matt said instead. "He's not doing his share of the work around here, but what else is new."

"Do you want me to speak to him about it?"

That was the last thing Matt wanted. "He's downtown."

"He's not . . ."

"I can hold my own with John," he cut in. He was surprised to find that although they were separated by thousands of miles, he still felt as if she were hovering over him.

"Mrs. Gannon sounded concerned when I talked with her yesterday."

"About what?" Perhaps it would have been better if he hadn't asked.

"She said there was a party the night we left, and you're both wandering around like Gypsies. She said you haven't changed your clothes since we left."

"Of course I have."

"What about the party?"

"John had some friends over."

"That doesn't sound like what she was talking about."

"We're fine, really, Mom."

For a moment he was afraid she was going to do something crazy, like fly home just to make sure he was telling the truth. But evidently his being there to answer the phone had helped to calm her fears.

"Is it hot in Paris?" he asked.

"Very."

"Have you sat out in any cafés?"

"A few, dear." She was saying something to someone else. His father?

"Matt?"

"Still here."

"Your father wants to know if you've mowed the lawn."

"Three days ago. I'll catch it again early next week. It rained here yesterday."

"Well, I'd better hang up. These calls are expensive." But it was clear that she wanted to go on talking, that she needed some further reassurance.

"Okay, Mom," he said. "I've got clothes in the dryer I'd better take out before they wrinkle." He thought this was a nice touch, domestic and dependable.

"All right, dear." But she didn't hang up.

He wanted to say, Go on, enjoy your trip, you've waited all your life to go to Europe. I'm fine, there's something new happening in my life but I don't want to talk about it . . .

Instead, he said, "I love you, Mom."

He almost heard her smile. "And I love you, too, dear. Good-bye till Sunday. We'll call again then."

"Good-bye."

After she hung up, he put the phone down slowly. Okay, he thought. That's done, that went all right. He returned to the back room and pulled the clothes from the dryer and more or less folded them in five minutes. On his way out the side door he heard John's window open above him.

"Did the good little mama's boy have a nice talk on the telephone?"

Matt looked up at his brother, who was leaning on his windowsill. "I told her you were bringing girls into the house, and she's flying home tonight."

"What?" John pressed his face against the screen. "You told her what?"

Matt hid his laughter by running for his bike. John was still yelling at him as he bumped down the driveway into the street.

He rode into the barrens and left his bike leaning against a tree. Yesterday's rain was already drying under the hot July sun. He smelled the turpentine aroma of the trees as he ran along one of the dirt roads; he felt the packed sand beneath his running shoes. In the field insects sang from their hiding places in the tall grass.

He called to Andrea as he approached the boathouse. She met him at the porch door. On the deck a towel was spread in the sun. Another towel was hanging over the railing at the water's edge.

"I thought you weren't coming," she said. She was wearing a long-sleeved white shirt over her wet bathing suit, the sleeves rolled up to her elbows, the front of the shirt open. He noticed how brown her tan looked against the blinding white of her shirt.

Behind her on the table her sketch pad lay open. On a chair she had arranged flowers in a vase.

"I had to wait for a phone call," he told her.

"I thought we could go for a swim," she said. "I went in without you when I got tired of waiting. It's hot."

He avoided the subject of swimming by stepping inside the porch to look more closely at her flower drawing. "That's good," he told her.

She reached from behind him to flip the sketch pad closed. "It's late. Want to go for a quick swim before I have to go up to the house?'"

He forced a nonchalant shrug. "I didn't bring my suit."

"So swim in your underwear. I'm a big girl."

"How's your father?" he asked quickly.

"Fine."

If he could have said let's go, and torn off his clothing to dive with her into the lake, then everything would have been fine. Playing like seals, splashing like five-year-olds, they would quickly have forgotten this tense moment. But this escape was denied him, and he could not find another.

"If you're angry because I was so late . . ."

"I'm not angry."

But it was plain she was. Because of what had happened last night? Today she had a shell built up around her that was a foot thick and made of hard glass.

"I've got to go," she said. Her father's bell had not yet begun to ring.

"Don't. I just got here."

"I really have to." She picked up her drawing materials and the vase of flowers.

"What about tonight?"

"What about it?"

"Well." He tried to think of something enticing. "We could go to a movie. They're showing *Gone With the Wind* downtown."

"I've seen it three times."

"Funny, I've never seen it."

"You should go, then." She backed out through the door and tried to pick up her towels. She dropped her box of pencils.

He picked them up for her and then loaded everything into her arms so that she could make it up the hill, even though this would only speed her on her way. Why did he always have to be so polite?

"Tonight," he said. "We could have a cookout right here. I'll bring everything."

She shook her head. A thick strand of her dark hair dropped in front of her face. She tried to toss it back, but that only brought down more. Before he could stop himself, he reached out and brushed the hair out of her eyes.

"I really have to eat with my father," she said, more gently.

"Eat light, save some of your appetite, and meet me down here whenever you get free."

She finally smiled. It lit up her whole face. "God, you're persistent."

"That's my middle name. Matthew Persistent Zaharis. It's from the Italian side of the family."

Then she laughed and he knew he was on safe ground. "All right, Matthew Persistent, I'll come down tonight. But I'll have to wait until Daddy goes up to his room, so I'll be late and not very hungry."

He did not ask her why a girl who last winter had had a lover in Paris now had to sneak out at night behind her father's back. But he wondered about it.

"Okay?" she asked.

"Okay. Great. I'll be here."

And then she had to spoil it all by saying, "And wear cutoffs or your swimming trunks, or you'll be going into the lake naked."

John was gone when he got home that afternoon, but the house was as messy as before. Matt killed the whole afternoon cleaning the house from end to end, top to bottom, every room except John's. He knew it wasn't all his to do, but he also knew it wouldn't get done if he didn't do it.

He searched through the stacks of signs and advertising posters he had been collecting in his closet for years, and found one to put on John's bedroom door. After cutting off the part he didn't want, he tacked up what was left with two thin nails:

A DISNEY EXTRAVAGANZA!

At five o'clock Mrs. Gannon came by with a tuna casserole. John was still out. Mrs. Gannon stayed for nearly half an hour, during which time she managed to check out the whole downstairs. No doubt his mother would get a full report. No doubt it would surprise her.

He gave Mrs. Gannon a cup of tea. He thanked her three times for the tuna casserole. He promised, as she backed out the door, to stop by her house in the next day or two to get her recipe for eggplant Parmesan.

When she was gone, he pushed the tuna casserole into the refrigerator. In the meat tray he noticed two steaks.

It took him only a moment to pack the steaks with ice into a heavy plastic bag. He put the bag in his small backpack, then added a wedge of paper plates, some matches, two knives, two forks, salt, pepper, and two bottles of beer. He raced from the house, snatching his field glasses from the closet as he went out. John might have been planning on a nice steak dinner, but Mrs. Gannon's tuna casserole was going to be just fine for him.

After riding downtown on his bike, he bought a small, cheap grill, a bag of potato chips, and two apples at Antonio's Market, charging it all against the account his parents had set up for them before they left. He was out of town by six o'clock, far too early to be meeting Andrea but safe from any chance of running into John.

As he pedaled along the street beside the lake, Matt again could smell steaks cooking at several of the cottages. This time he gloated over the thought that he had steaks of his own; and he wove his way carelessly through the early evening traffic, already imagining how it would be to share them with Andrea.

# Chapter 9

*T*he evening was warm; sunlight lingered in the western sky. After he stashed all the food inside the porch of the boathouse, Matt took his field glasses and walked back into the woods.

Among the shadows that loomed across the sandy road, his feet made almost no sound. He thought, as he often did when out bird watching, of making himself disappear. If he could become as naturally a part of the pine barrens as the wind that slipped in among the trees from the lake, then no bird would fear him. He would be able to observe them unobserved; he would be nothing more than another shadow on the sandy road, a movement of a branch in the wind.

He liked the idea of invisibility. At times in his life it was his favorite fantasy. Invisible people could slip away and no one would notice they were gone.

The multicolored bird was perched on a branch high up in a large white pine. Searching the treetops with his field glasses, he saw it just as it left the branch to flutter off toward the lake, a flash of red against the glowing sky. He raced after it, running as silently as he could along the road, then onto the carpet of needles beneath the trees. He tried to keep the tiny speck in sight as he ducked under low branches. If only he could see where it next settled down to roost, if only he could know what sort of bird it was.

He ran across another rutted road, into a tangle of juniper bushes on the far side. Sharp needles raked his arms as he tried to squirm his way through. Too late, he realized it would have been quicker to run around the junipers.

The bird was gone, as if it had melted into the sky. The pungent smell of crushed juniper drifted up into his nose like incense. He pulled himself out of the bushes and, brushing off his clothes, walked slowly on toward the lake. Although he carefully searched the trees for another glimpse of the strange bird, he couldn't find it again.

But he believed in his heart that this was the same bird he had seen last week, the bird he had wanted to identify as a painted bunting, and would have, too, if only that were possible.

When darkness came he left the woods. Lights were on in the Staffords' house above the field. He wondered if Andrea, perhaps at the kitchen sink, looking out the window, might see him crossing through the grass to the boathouse.

He was sitting on the deck, his back against the porch, when she came down an hour later. He heard her first, the grass brushing against her as she came down the hill.

"Hi," he called, in case she hadn't seen him.

She sat down beside him on the deck. She had brought an open bottle of wine and two glasses. Without a word she poured them each a drink.

"Hungry?" he asked.

"Not really."

He could smell the soap she had used in the bath or shower she had taken today. It was as rich, as earthy a smell as the odor of the still-warm grass in the field close by.

"Wait till you see what I brought," he told her. "Then you'll be hungry."

He had already gathered small pieces of wood for his grill. As he struck a match to set the small bit of paper under the wood on fire, he could feel her watching him.

"Let's go for a swim first," she said.

"Let's eat first," he said quickly. He unwrapped the steaks and showed them to her. "I'm starved."

She didn't argue. As he cooked the steaks, she sat at the edge of the firelight eating potato chips and sipping her wine.

"How do you like your steak?"

She laughed. "How about burned on the outside and raw inside? That's how they're going to come out, right?"

He nodded. "I guess so. I should have bought some charcoal."

"Don't be silly. I happen to like my steaks that way."

He enjoyed it when she laughed, when they joked. Her darker moods made him uncomfortable.

He turned the two steaks carefully. The flames flew up

into his face as new fat dripped down into the fire.

"Were you bird watching?" she asked, noticing his field glasses for the first time.

He nodded. "Yeah, for a while." He told her about the strange bird he had now seen twice. "I still haven't had a real good look at it, but I've seen enough to know it doesn't match anything that should be around here."

"Maybe it's an escaped pet bird."

"I thought of that."

"And?"

"Maybe that's the explanation."

"But you'd rather it was wild, here by some fluke of the winds."

"Yeah." He looked at her face in the flickering light from the fire.

"Why?"

"Because I'd like it to be wild."

"But why?"

He looked down at the steaks. The flames were licking the fat along the edges. "If it's wild it can fly south before winter."

"So it won't die?"

"Yeah. And if it's wild, it's free. A pet bird isn't free even when it escapes."

"I see."

"Dinner's served," he said, pulling the steaks off the grill onto paper plates. As they ate, an orange moon rose above the eastern shore of the lake.

"Did you arrange for that?" Andrea asked.

Matt looked across the lake. "Sure. Got to have a moon."

"You're funny," she said.

"Funny ha-ha or funny wacko?" he asked.

She didn't answer.

"It makes a difference," he said finally.

"Why did you want so badly for us to have a cookout tonight?" she asked.

They were sitting back against the porch watching the last smoke curl up from the grill into the moonlight.

"I don't know," he said.

"You know. You're just not saying."

"Maybe."

They were sitting so close he could feel the warmth of her skin. When he turned around to kiss her, he banged into her nose. He went ahead with the kiss anyway. For a moment her mouth was soft against his, then she pushed him away.

"You're too young," she said.

He slumped back onto the deck. "No, I'm not. You're not all that much older than me."

"That's what you think."

"You're seventeen," he guessed.

"Wrong again." She stood up suddenly and pulled off her dress. She was wearing her bathing suit under it. "Come on, let's go for a swim."

"We just ate."

She pulled him up onto his feet, then walked along the deck toward the edge where the water was deepest. He followed her, but not too closely.

"Come on!"

"No, really, we just ate a big meal."

At the edge of the deck she turned to face him, her hands on her hips. "God, you should hear yourself. It sounds like your mother has got you totally brainwashed."

"It's not that."

"Did you wear something to swim in?"

"No."

"Afraid to show me your legs?"

"No, of course not."

"Bet you are," she said and spun into a dive that hardly rippled the water as she went in. She came up pulling her hair out of her eyes. "Come in, Matt. It's lovely! You can see the moonlight under the water."

He shook his head, but forced himself to stand as close to the edge of the deck as he dared, his left hand tightly clutching the last rotten post of the railing. Every time he looked down into the water he felt a dizzy ache in his head that got louder and louder.

Andrea swam at the edge of his vision. Her legs kicked strongly. They flipped up into the air whenever she dove into the depths. He wiped sweat out of his eyes with his free hand and hoped the moonlight wouldn't reveal to her the look that must have been on his face.

At last she climbed back onto the deck and stood beside him, dripping a steady stream of water onto the planks. She tried to wipe the water out of her eyes with wet fingers.

"It's wonderful in there tonight," she said. Like swimming in some kind of dream, with the moonlight all around and the . . ."

The moment she touched his back he knew what she was doing. He tried to bring his other hand around to grab the post, but he was already losing his balance as she pushed. He fell over the yawning pit of the water, fell toward the black lake that was rushing up to meet him. He flailed now at the air, as if that might be solid enough to stop him, but it wasn't, how could it be? And he heard himself scream.

The water was cold. He seemed to go down a long, long way, but he knew that wasn't true, because he was already reaching for the edge of the deck above him, digging his nails into the splintery wood, kicking at the water with his legs the way you might kick at a monster in a dream, trying to push it as far away from you as you could.

His fingers ripped at the edge of the deck. He was afraid that if he lost his hold now, he would never come up out of that cold water again. His fingers found the far edge of a plank, a half-inch of leverage. It was enough. He clawed his way up, driving his knees against the wood, pulling against the heavy drag of his soaked clothing. Then he was up on the deck and running, his shoes making strange squeaking sounds against the planks as he pushed by Andrea, her face white in the moonlight, her arms trying to stop him. But he got past her and ran off the deck and into the grass and deeper into the grass until he found a place where he could hide.

Andrea was calling to him. Far off through the grass he heard her shouting his name. Slowly she came closer. Feeling shame deeper than any he had ever known in his life before, he stood up in the grass to face her.

"Matt," she said when she saw him. "Oh Matt, I'm sorry. I didn't know, I had no idea . . ."

She had put on her dress and it clung to her wet skin. In the moonlight her hair had a sharp edge. He walked by her on his way back to the boathouse.

"I should have told you," he mumbled. He paused to pull a splinter from his palm. "I should have told you."

She insisted they build a fire on the beach just north of the boathouse and try to dry his clothes. He pulled off his jeans and shirt, and they dragged some branches close to the fire to make a drying rack. The arrangement fell over twice before they got it propped up sufficiently to hold the weight of his wet clothes. Andrea sat near him on the rocks, holding his hands, rubbing his wrists.

"Move closer to the fire," she said. "Don't get chilled."

"I'm all right." He had broken two of his fingernails in his scramble to get out of the water. He tried now to ignore the pain.

"You're shivering."

"So what? I'm not a goddamn baby."

She looked away.

"I'm sorry," he said. "I feel like a jerk, that's all." Steam was rising from his jeans. He got up to pull them back from the fire, which was roaring its way through a crate they had found near the edge of the beach.

"I've always been scared of the water," he told her, not looking in her direction. "I nearly drowned when I was four, and I haven't gone into the water since, until tonight."

"That must be a terrible memory," she said. "How did it happen?"

He shrugged and sat down beside her again. "It's not a memory. I don't know a thing about it except what my parents have told me. I slipped under while we were all at the beach one summer day. The water was crowded, all kinds of kids splashing around and raising hell. By the time they missed me and dragged me out, I was unconscious."

The fire snapped and popped, sending up a curtain of sparks.

"Can you ever forgive me?" she asked. She was crying.

"Sure," he said. "Sure. You didn't know. You were just having some fun."

Her crying opened up a deep feeling of sadness inside him. He wondered where it came from. "Stop crying," he said, his voice hoarse. "It's nothing."

"I could help you get over it," she said, staring at the fire. "I know I could."

He shrugged. "Why bother? As long as I avoid anything deeper than rain puddles, I'll be fine."

Above them from the top of the hill her father's bell began to ring. Looking up at the house, Matt searched in vain for a light in any of the windows, then realized that of course there wouldn't be any light for a blind man.

"I *could* help you," Andrea said again.

The bell rang on and on, altering the night, but they stayed by the fire as long as they could.

# Chapter 10

"**W**e could use desensitizing techniques to get you over your fear of the water," Andrea told him the next morning.

He looked at her from his perch on top of the picnic table. She was sitting in a chair at the far end of the porch, sketching him in pencil in her pad.

"What's that?"

"Desensitizing. That's how they cure phobics."

"Who's *they*?"

"Psychiatrists. You know, shrinks."

"And I'm a phobic?"

"Hold still." She looked at him, then down at the pad on her knees. "You're sexy, do you know?"

He was not going to be distracted, even by a compliment he'd never expected to hear from any girl. "You said I'm a phobic."

She smiled. "It's not a dirty word."

"What is it, then?"

"Just someone like you who has an extreme fear of

something ordinary, like heights or closets or spiders. You know." She turned one of the pencils on edge and rubbed it heavily into one side of the drawing. "I'm really inspired today. This is *good*." She looked up again. "Can I draw you in the nude sometime?"

He felt his face grow warm. "I'd be embarrassed."

She laughed. "Really?"

"Tell me about desensitizing."

"Well, basically," she said, peering intently at his face, then returning to her drawing, "all they do, the shrinks, I mean, is expose a phobic little by little to the thing he or she is afraid of, a little more each time, until the fear is overcome."

"How do you know all this?"

"I read every psych book I could get my hands on a few years ago. I was going to be the new Anna Freud."

"What changed your mind?"

Andrea shrugged. "I lost interest."

"Why?"

"Stop moving around."

"Why did you lose interest?"

"God, you're persistent."

"You said that yesterday."

She stopped drawing. "I guess I did."

He sensed that she was trying to avoid giving him a direct answer. "I didn't mean to be nosy."

"Of course you did. You want to know everything about me." She picked up another pencil and resumed work on the sketch.

"Well, that's normal, isn't it?"

"What?"

"To want to know about you."

"I guess." She looked up at him, then back at her pad. "I lost interest in psychiatry because my own therapy didn't turn out so good."

"You were . . ."

"I wasn't a raving lunatic, if that's what you're thinking." She broke the point on the pencil she was using, selected another. "I was just in therapy for a while, that's all."

He waited for her to go on, but she didn't. "How long does this desensitizing take?" he asked finally.

"Months, maybe longer."

He looked out through the screens at the lake. "Months?"

"Hold still!"

"Months?"

"Well, a shrink would also be digging into your head. You know, trying to find out what your fears are based on."

"We already know why I'm afraid of the water."

Andrea looked up and nodded. "That's right, we do."

His hands were sweating. He tried to wipe them on his jeans without being obvious about it. "Too bad there aren't any shrinks in Bredstone."

"Desensitizing is just a technique. Anyone can do it. You just take the thing a phobic is afraid of and divide it up into little pieces, little stages he can tackle one at a time."

"Were you a phobic?"

"No." She looked up from her pad. "The water we need is right out there."

"I was afraid you were going to say that."

She didn't smile. Her eyes seemed like pools of brown fire, growing larger as he stared into them. "I'd be with you every step of the way."

He shook his head. "Let's see the sketch."

She got up from the chair and walked to the table to give him the pad. She had caught his likeness. But there was something wrong with it. He stared down at the pad for a long time before he realized what had happened.

"You hate it," she said.

"No, it's good, only . . ."

"Only what?"

"I look scared."

She took back the pad and studied the drawing. Slowly she nodded. "You're right. I'm sorry."

He slid off the table. "Don't worry about it. It's true. I am scared."

"We'd go very slowly."

He looked out at the lake, suddenly wishing he lived in the middle of a desert. Now, sand was something he could roll around in with no trouble at all.

"Let me help you," she said in a low voice.

"Why?"

"Because I'd like to . . . because I know . . ."

She shrugged her shoulders, leaving her thought incomplete.

He wanted to say no but he was ashamed of his fear, ashamed to admit he didn't even want to try to overcome it.

"You could go very slowly," she said.

They left the boathouse and walked up to the beach

where they had built the fire last night to dry his clothes. Ten feet from the water's edge, they stopped.

"Take off your shoes and roll up your jeans."

"Easy for you to say," he mumbled.

She kicked off her own shoes. Slowly he followed suit. The water seemed suddenly closer, although they hadn't taken another step toward it.

She took his hand. "We'll just walk in up to our calves, no farther. We'll stand there a few seconds, then we'll come out."

"I didn't bring my beach pail," he said.

He expected her to make a face at him, tell him to cut out the feeble jokes. But she didn't. She seemed to understand how he used these jokes to prop up his courage.

She tugged on his hand. "Come on, Matt. Now."

"Well, okay, just so we can go on holding hands." He tried to laugh, but the sound he made was more like a wheeze.

At the water's edge his toes dug into the coarse sand. She had an arm around his waist now. He felt like a little kid.

"Up to our calves, right?"

She nodded. "And then right out again."

"And that's going to do it?"

"Not in one day, but in time."

"Do I get a kiss after I go in?"

"We'll see."

That was exactly what his mother would have said. Furious with her, and with himself for his foolish jokes, he pulled away from her and walked three steps into the water. Every cell in his body cringed, every muscle tried to turn him around and force him to run the other way. He took two more steps, then two more. When he felt the cold water curling around his legs near the middle of his calves, he turned to face her.

"Gutsy, huh?" He swallowed hard as his stomach threatened to heave up breakfast. "All I need is a cape and I could save the world."

She started to say something, but he shook his head. "Don't say it. I know how impressed you are."

"Stop it."

He splashed back onto the beach, his legs suddenly so weak under him he thought he might fall. "What the world needs is more of that kind of courage."

"It was courage," she said softly.

"Bullshit."

"Don't hate yourself."

"I . . ." His eyes were burning with tears. "I have to keep doing this?" he asked.

She nodded.

And then she tackled him, knocking him over onto the sand. She pressed her face against his ear. "It *was* courage," she whispered.


He waded in three more times that first morning, and the next day he managed to go out a little farther. On the third day he wore his cutoffs and predicted he was going to swim into water over his head. But he didn't.

"This isn't getting any easier," he said.

"It won't, for a while."

He tried four times to get out to the depth of his knees. "I can't," he said at last.

"Tomorrow."

"And what if I can't tomorrow?"

"Then the day after."

He sat on the boathouse deck and watched her swim off the deep end. She looked like some sort of frolicking fish. He felt a stab of envy that opened up all kinds of longings inside him.

"Isn't it enough you're rich and pretty?" was all he managed to say about it when she came out of the water and sat down beside him.

She paused from drying her hair to look at him. "What made you say that just now?"

He shrugged. "Do you have to be Olympic material too?"

"You think I've got it made, don't you?"

He nodded. "You do."

She shook her head. "You don't really know me at all."

The next day they went looking for his brightly colored bird. He had gone into the water as far as his knees, and he was feeling proud of himself.

The air was hot under the trees; no birds were stirring. They sat on a rock and took turns sweeping a thick grove of bushes with his field glasses.

"You don't remember anything about the time you almost drowned?" she asked suddenly. "When you were four."

Startled, he took back the glasses and refocused them for his eyes. "Nothing."

"Have you tried?"

"Well, four was not a big year for me. I don't remember much about anything else that year."

"You were playing in the water?"

"Sure, I guess." He kept the field glasses to his eyes even though nothing was moving in the thicket.

"Then what happened?"

"I was playing and he grabbed me and then I must have gone under the surface, only I just don't remember any of it at all."

"Who grabbed you?"

"What?"

"You said someone grabbed you."

"No, I didn't."

"Yes, you did."

"You're crazy."

"You said someone grabbed you."

He put down the glasses and looked at her. "Why the hell would I say that when I don't remember a damn thing about it?"

"I don't know, Matt," she said. She stood up. "Let's go back to the boathouse."

Before they reached the field they could hear her father's bell ringing up at the house.

"There he goes again," Matt said.

"Yeah." The word came out flat and hard, as if it were a cap to hold down something else. She put her hands on his waist. "See you tomorrow?"

He nodded. "How about tonight?"

"We have friends coming for dinner."

The sound of the bell faded as a gust of wind blew across the field, but then it returned. "You'd better go," he said at last.

"I keep hoping he'll find his way into that big poem he needs for his book and ease up on me and on himself." She looked away.

"No luck yet?"

"No, none at all. He sits at his desk playing with his tape recorder every day until he can't stand it any longer, waiting for the dam to break, and it never does."

Matt looked across the blue surface of the lake. "I know how he feels."

During the following days Matt worked his way deeper into the water, to above his knees, then to the middle of his thighs. The one thing that never changed was the fear: He pushed right up to the edge of it every day and could only step into deeper water by risking a return of the blind panic that had so devastated him the night Andrea pushed him off the boathouse deck.

What kept him going was the fact that Andrea's technique seemed to be working. Maybe he was just as afraid now as when he started, but he was farther into the water than he had been at any time since he was four.

If you didn't count the time she pushed him in. He preferred not to think about that.

On the evening of the day he went into the water up to his waist, they celebrated by going to the movies. She came by the house in the Mercedes to pick him up. He was disappointed John was nowhere around, because he secretly wanted to show off a little, show John that he had a girl friend of his own.

After the movie they went to Bob and Jerry's for a pizza. They were still arguing about the film, which Matt had enjoyed and Andrea had hated.

"It was so contrived," Andrea kept saying. "The plot was full of holes big enough to drive a truck through."

"What holes?" he asked as they waited for their pizza.

She made a face. "Like the way none of the friends thought their little blackmail scheme might backfire. I knew right away it would blow up in their faces."

"I suppose."

"And some of the dialogue. Nobody talks like that."

"Sure they do. I talk like that."

"No, you don't."

"All the time."

"Matt, you *don't* talk the way they talked in that movie."

"Sure. I'm always telling you how much I love the rain, and how lonely it gets at three in the morning when the gin bottle is empty."

She laughed.

"I liked it."

"What was there to like?"

"It made me feel things. And the ending was so exciting I almost . . ."

"You almost jumped into my lap."

He nodded. "So it had to be doing something right, because I'm a very sophisticated movie critic. I saw *Bambi* twice."

His brother was coming in the front door of the restaurant with Michele. Matt nudged Andrea.

"That's my brother, John."

She turned to look. John nodded as he and Michele took a table on the other side of the dining room. Michele ignored them.

"Friendly," Andrea said.

"Really. My family is very close. We love each other so much we . . ."

The waitress brought their pizza. Matt realized Andrea was looking around for a knife and fork. "You eat it with your hands," he told her.

"I know that," she said.

They each took a slice. Andrea held hers so that she could blow on it. "*Do* you get lonely at three in the morning?"

He had to think for a moment to remember what she was talking about. "Sure," he said. "Don't you?"

She took a bite and nodded.

They drove through Bredstone for a while, doing the grand tour. Then she took him home. He was surprised to find John back already, lying on the wicker couch on the porch with a beer can resting on his chest.

"Tender parting scene," John said. "I thought you two were never going to break it up."

Matt walked through the porch into the house. John got up and followed him.

"So that's the heartthrob in little brother's life."

Matt searched the refrigerator for a bottle of Coke.

"You didn't have to spy on us."

"I wasn't spying. Besides, the way you two were looking at each other over at Bob and Jerry's, you're not going to be a secret for long."

"Where's Michele?" Matt asked, to change the subject. He dumped ice into a glass and poured his Coke.

"Had to crash early." John swung a kitchen chair around and sat on it backwards. "Tell me, little brother, is it the pig in her that you like so much, or do you just dig that Mercedes she drives?"

Matt stared into his glass. "She isn't a pig," he said in a low voice.

John laughed. "Oh, she's a pig all right. I'm an expert on pigs. My school is full of them." He leaned on the back of the chair. "Hey, don't get me wrong. Pigs serve a big purpose in life. Only I just thought you of all people would want something a little more . . ."

Matt threw his glass. It spun by John's head, splashing his face with Coke before it hit the wall behind the stove.

For a moment the only sound was the glass breaking, pieces raining down onto the floor. Then John's chair fell over as he tackled Matt. They landed together on the floor, swinging punches at each other as they rolled up against the table. Matt tasted blood. It was running from his nose into his mouth.

He fought doggedly, but John ended up on top of him, holding him down, punching his nose, his eyes, the top of his head. Matt tried to squirm free. From the floor, his own punches carried no weight, were doing no damage.

He was coughing, gasping for air, drowning in his

own blood. Buried under John's weight, he kicked hard to free himself. He was drowning, drowning . . .

And when it came to him, he was so struck by the picture of it that he stopped fighting: the blue sky, the blue water, the look on John's face then, the water in his eyes, the sky gone, the silver bubbles, *his* bubbles, rising away from him higher and higher as John pushed him under and held him there, fingers like wire around his arms, on his shoulders.

"Had enough?"

John was still sitting on him, his fist raised to come down again. Matt looked up and focused his eyes on the face he had hated like no other face for so long.

"It was you, you bastard!"

John punched him again. "Enough?"

Matt spit at him. It only brought more punches, but he didn't care. Now he knew.

# Chapter 11

$J$ohn eventually got tired of the one-sided fight and let him up. Matt went to the sink and washed the blood off his face.

"You okay?"

Matt ignored the question. When he was done washing up, he got a broom and dug out the pieces of glass from behind the stove.

"You had it coming, shithead."

Matt dropped the broken glass into the wastebasket. Then he went up to his room and filled his backpack with clothes, squeezing in his journal and a handful of paperback books.

Downstairs John was still in the kitchen, drinking a beer. When he saw the backpack, he put the beer can down on the table.

"Where are you headed for?"

Matt went to the closet for his field glasses. He slung them around his neck, then tightened the straps on his pack.

"I said where the hell are you going?"

He stepped around John and went out the side door, expecting another punch, but none came. He took his bike from the garage and rode down into the street.

During the ride to the pine barrens, he kept his attention on the late-night traffic. Headlights burned his eyes; summer kids in the back of a pickup truck shouted obscenities at him.

But he paid them no mind. They couldn't touch him tonight. When he reached the barrens, he pedaled off the pavement onto the sand. He wheeled his bike the rest of the way, under trees that whispered softly to him in the night wind.

There were no lights on up at Andrea's house, but across the lake Point Rollins was outlined in tiny silver beads. On the porch of the boathouse he dropped his backpack on the floor and sat down in one of the chairs. Small waves beat against the far side of the deck — a sound that might have soothed him tonight, had he been able to listen to it.

But he was far away and only four years old, remembering the way it felt to die.

Andrea found him lying on the deck in the morning sun, trying to drive the dawn chill from his bones.

"Matt!" she said. "I saw your bike, but it's so . . ." When she noticed his face, she stopped. He turned away. She crouched beside him on the deck. "What happened?"

He shrugged. He touched the swollen place near his mouth. "Had a little fight with John." He had washed his face carefully in the lake water early this morning, but that did not stop Andrea from taking a corner of her shirt, dipping it into the water, and going after the cuts near his left eye herself.

"Hold still."

"That hurts."

"I imagine it does." The look on her face betrayed her casual tone of voice. "Why did he beat you so?"

"He didn't beat me. We had a fight."

"About what?"

Matt sidestepped telling her what had started his quarrel with John the night before. "I remembered when I was four and he tried to drown me by holding me under the water." He grabbed her hand so that she couldn't wipe his face anymore. "I remembered the whole thing while we were fighting last night."

She did not seem surprised. They stared at each other for a long time. "Poor John," she said at last.

He shook his head. "What do you mean, poor John? He tried to . . ."

"Sssh, I know." She pressed her fingers gently to his mouth to shut him up.

She didn't say anything more about it, but sat down on the deck beside him, holding his hand on her lap. "Have you been here all night?"

He nodded. He looked over the trees beyond her house, at the round dome of Firetop Mountain, almost hidden behind the green slash of an intervening ridge. "There's a shelter up on Firetop. I can go camp up there."

"Firetop?"

He pointed to the mountain.

"You can't go home?"

He shook his head. "I'm not going to live with that bastard."

She bit her lip, as if to stop herself from arguing with him. "Why go up on that mountain?"

"It's nice up there. It's quiet and peaceful and there's no one to hassle you."

"You really like being alone, don't you?"

"Sometimes."

She held up his hand, looking at the lines on his palm. "Stay here at the boathouse," she said in a low voice. "That way you won't be so far away." She seemed to be finding something important on his palm. She held it more tightly. "I can bring you blankets later, and sneak you down your meals."

"What about your father?"

She dropped his hand and brushed impatiently at her hair. "He'll never know you're here."

He considered it. "Okay," he said.

"You can still be alone as much as you want," she said.

He thought of several replies, but the moment for them quickly passed.

"Come on," she said. "Time for your morning swim."

Thinking back on the morning from a vantage point later in the day, Matt wondered if they had both thought the same thing: that having remembered the details of his near-drowning at four, he would now be able to march into the water and swim a hundred yards. Neither of them announced this possibility, this hope. But he realized later that he had felt it, and he sensed that Andrea had felt it too.

She had driven him into the water with a special urgency.

But nothing this simple occurred. Matt forced himself into the water up to his waist, as he had yesterday. Then the wall of fear met him head-on.

"Now try to float," Andrea said beside him. "Just lean forward with your arms out and your head down."

He looked at the water. His legs were trembling; he was in too far already.

"Don't fight it," Andrea was saying, her voice faint and distant despite the fact she was standing there next to him. "Just relax. Just let go."

Staring down into the water, Matt felt himself beginning to lose his balance. Whirling suddenly, he splashed his way to shore. Andrea stayed in the water. If she was disappointed, she hid it well.

"Come on," she said. "Try again."

Three more times he walked out waist deep, staring into water as gray as the edge of night; then he ran from the sickening vertigo that threatened to pull him down under the surface.

"I can't," he said finally, and walked back to the boat-house.

When she sat down beside him, he told her, as a joke, "Maybe I should drink six beers and throw myself off the edge of the deck."

She shook her head. "No, that's the worst thing you could do."

"I know. I know."

She picked up his hand and pressed the back of it against her mouth. "We'll beat this thing," she said.

He wondered why it meant so much to her. It seemed as if she had turned this into a personal cause.

"We can do it," she repeated.

She had sounded so sure they would. Long after his own faith had washed away in the cold lake water, he still kept trying, wading out each day because *she* was so sure he could conquer his fear. Long after he had disappointed himself, giving up somewhere deep inside, he kept on going through the motions, in order not to disappoint her.

Then one day she said, suddenly very angry, "You're not trying!"

He looked at her. She had already been in for a swim, and her dark hair was wrapped tightly around her head. She stood in the water with her hands on her hips. "You're not, Matt."

"Yes, I am."

"No. You've given up."

"Like hell." His anger was all the stronger because she had somehow guessed the truth. Instead of going in deeper, he waded back to the beach. "I haven't given up. It's just . . ."

"Just what?" She waded through the water toward him.

"It's going to take something more now. To float, I mean."

She nodded. "It is. So what are you waiting for, a comet in the sky?" She joined him on the beach and tried to pull him in again.

He pulled away. "I can't let go. I don't trust myself to float."

"You haven't tried."

Rage choked him. "Go to hell."

"I mean it, Matt." They looked at each other for a long time. "Maybe we should stop trying," she said finally, looking away.

It was what he had wanted to say himself, to call a halt to this daily torture. But hearing her say it now frightened him, and he told her quickly, "No, we just need a break, that's all."

"Really?" She sounded skeptical.

"Yeah, a break, a goddamn day off, that's all."

She shrugged her shoulders.

"I'm not going to quit."

"You have already."

"Then I'll unquit."

"Sure."

He clenched his hands into fists. "You think I'm a coward, don't you?"

She shook her head. "No, I don't."

"Yes, you do."

"Oh, Matt, what does it matter what *I* think? It's what you think about yourself that matters."

He looked up at Firetop Mountain. All he could see of it from the beach was the highest rock face gleaming in the sunlight. "Let's take a day off."

"And do what?"

He nodded toward the mountain. "Go for a hike, up Firetop. Let's get as far away from this damn lake as we can, just for one day."

112

Was he pleading with her? If he was, she took pity on him and did not make him continue to beg.

"All right," she said.

That afternoon he went back to the house to get his hiking boots. It was the first time he had returned home since the fight with John. There was a note for him on the refrigerator:

> *Mom called again last night. I'm getting*
> *sick of telling her you're okay.*

Matt turned the paper over and wrote:

> *Tell her to call me at my new address.*

But he didn't write down where he was staying.

He took as many clean clothes as he could squeeze into his backpack, along with everything he and Andrea would need for their hike. Tying the laces of his boots together, he slung them over his shoulder. He was closing the side door when he heard a car behind him. Turning, he watched John drive up beside the house.

There was a long crease in the side of the car, and one of the headlights was smashed.

"What the hell did you do?"

John shrugged. "Went off the road up on Point Rollins."

"Dad's going to love it."

"I'll have it fixed before they get back."

"That's good." Matt went to his bike and pushed up the kickstand.

"We still got the house to paint," John said.

"Fine. You tell me when you want to start and I'll be here."

"How about tomorrow?"

"I can't tomorrow."

John grunted something under his breath.

Matt swung onto his bike. "I can't tomorrow, that's all there is to it."

"Okay, day after."

Matt nodded.

"Where the hell are you staying?" John asked before he could ride off. "I've been checking all over."

Matt was surprised that John had bothered to look for him. "I'm at the lake," he said as he rode quickly out into the street.

Andrea came down through the wet morning grass early the next day. He looked at her sneakers.

"You're going to wear those?"

"Sure. I don't need crampons and an ice ax, do I?"

"No, but you should wear hiking boots."

"I don't have hiking boots." She looked at him. "Do you want your breakfast, or shall I pitch it out into the lake?"

"No, come on." He grabbed the package out of her hand. "What is it?"

"Fried egg on toast. At least it was on the toast when I wrapped it up." She had brought a thermos of coffee also, and as he poured a cup, steam fanned out above his hands.

Andrea turned to look at the top of the mountain peeping over the edge of the ridge. "It looks a long way off."

"We can drive to the lodge. Most of the trails leave from there."

"Okay," she said.

As they walked up to the car, Matt glanced at the house.

"Is your father writing this morning?"

Andrea shrugged. "He's finished the articles. There's nothing left now but the poem. And that still won't come."

On the ride over the back roads to the lodge, Matt reached for the canvas shoulder bag Andrea was bringing with her.

"Get out of there."

"I'm just seeing what you brought for lunch."

She snatched the bag out of his hands and threw it onto the back seat. "It won't be lunch if you eat it now."

There were no other cars parked at the lodge. A board was nailed across the front door. All the panes of glass in the top-floor windows were broken.

"People don't stay here anymore?" Andrea asked as they got out of the car and pulled out their gear.

Matt shook his head. "No, not now. It used to be a ski lodge." He looked at the deserted building. "That was years ago, before the mountains further north put up their big lifts and started making snow and building condos. Nobody comes here in the winter now. Who wants to carry skis all the way up a mountain when you can ride a lift?"

She held his backpack for him. "What do you have in here? It weighs a ton."

He shrugged into the shoulder straps. "Nothing much.

115

Extra clothes in case we get cold, socks, spare pair of shoes, coil of rope . . ."

She looked at him. "We're not doing any rock climbing."

"No, but you should have a rope along just in case."

"In case of what?"

"I don't know. Just in case." He showed her how to clip the canteen onto her belt. "Suppose you stumble and twist your ankle."

"Suppose I do. You'll use the rope to truss me up like a chicken and carry me down?"

"No, I'll use the rope to rig the rain tarp to cover you while I go for help."

"God!"

"Never mind," he said. "I just like to be prepared. I hike by myself a lot. If something happens, I've got no one to turn to. If I don't have it with me, I don't have it."

The trails all started from a main junction a few hundred yards from the lodge. Andrea glanced back several times at the derelict building.

"It looks haunted."

"Used to be a real party place, but it doesn't look like much now."

They took the main trail to the first bridge. On the other side of Barley Brook the weathered signboards pointed in three directions. The Hunt Trail followed the stream to the right, and this was the direction Matt chose. As they followed the trail and the stream up toward the head of the valley, Matt walked behind Andrea, watching her nimble footwork on the slippery rocks.

"You've climbed before," he said.

"Not really. Just a little hiking."

"Where?"

"In the French Alps."

He was glad that he was behind her, so that she couldn't see his face. "Then how come you don't have hiking boots?" he asked.

"I haven't done any hiking since I was a kid." She turned to look at him. "What's the matter?"

"I sounded like a real jerk back there, didn't I? Lecturing you on equipment."

"No, you sounded very correct and concerned."

"Sure. But you're the one who's been to the Alps. All I've ever climbed . . ."

"This isn't a competition, Matt," she said.

"No, but . . ."

She stopped to put her hands on her hips, pushing back the shoulder bag to get it out of her way. "You don't have to prove anything."

Above them the treetops billowed in the wind. He was very conscious of how close they were, standing there on the trail above the stream. He could smell her hair.

"Relax," she whispered. "Let's leave all *that* down there." She waved vaguely toward the trail junction behind them, but she didn't explain what *that* was. He thought of the lake, though, and his failure to let go in the water and float.

"Yeah," he said bitterly, "let's leave that behind."

It was a warm day. They didn't reach the wind until

they'd climbed up one wall of the valley into a hardwood forest that stretched across a ridge toward the main thrust of the mountain itself. Through the trees they caught occasional glimpses of the dome of Firetop; it still looked high and remote above them.

"There was a fire here about a hundred years ago," he told her. "It burned over the whole top of the mountain, and then erosion took off the soil. That's why it's so bare up there now."

"Hence the name Firetop."

He nodded. "Right."

They paused for a drink in a small clearing in the forest. The ground here was soft and wet. She handed him the canteen. She had pulled out the ends of her plaid shirt and tied them in a knot across her stomach. Her face glowed with sweat.

He drank heavily and gave her back the canteen. "There's a spring farther up. We'll fill it again there."

Below the first outcropping of rock, the trail became very steep. Tree roots formed a ladder up the hillside. He stayed close behind her, ready to steady her if she slipped, but she climbed quickly and surely into the sunlight above. Pausing on the rocks, they had their first view, to the south and west over the hills that rolled away toward the state line.

"It's lovely," she said, breathing hard. "How far can we see?"

He squinted into the distance. "Maybe fifty miles."

They lingered on the rocks, then plunged down with the trail into a dark forest of stunted spruce trees. The narrow trail wound through the trees to a small pool that emerged from under a boulder the size of a three-story house. Andrea stared up at it as Matt refilled the canteen.

"It must have rolled down the mountain a long time ago," he told her. "It's a wonder it ever stopped here." He stood up and gave her the canteen to drink from. He watched the rivulets of water run down her chin onto her bare throat.

She gasped at last and handed him the canteen. "That's wonderful water."

"Like nothing you'll find down below."

Just above the spring the trail passed close to a log lean-to with a metal roof. A chipmunk ran under the building with a sharp whistle of alarm.

Andrea stopped to look at the shelter. "Is this the place you were going to camp out in?"

He nodded. He looked for signs of recent campfires but found none.

"It's kind of lonesome," she said.

He didn't reply. He walked up to the lean-to and sat down in the open side. Andrea stood a few feet away, looking at him.

"Are we resting?"

He nodded, then smiled when she smiled. "Sure, let's take a break." He slipped out of his pack; it fell over onto the floor of the shelter with a dull thump. "I want to tell you about this place. I'm just working up my courage."

She sat down beside him and pulled back her hair with both hands. "Is it something bad?"

"No." He shook his head. "No, it's something good.

119

Only I've never told anyone before. Promise you won't laugh?"

She was looking up at the trees. "I won't laugh."

"When I was eight I got lost up here. My father was into hiking then. He wanted us to do all the mountains around here. This was our first real climb. Turned out to be our last, too."

"Your whole family got lost?"

He shook his head. "No, just me. But everybody started out. Mom and Dad, me and brother John."

"What happened?"

"We came up the Needle Pond Trail. We stopped to picnic in a meadow about even with here but over on the other side of the mountain. My mother was too tired to go off bird watching with me, so I went alone. I was supposed to stay close, but of course I didn't." He shook his head. "I was feeling like Mr. Big, up here on my first real mountain, and before I knew it I had no idea where the meadow was or where I was."

Andrea moved closer and put her hand on his knee. "What did you do?"

Matt laughed. "Cried a lot." He was still sweating, even though they had been resting for some time now. "Ran around in circles, cried some more. Got mad at my mother because she didn't come find me. You know, kid stuff like that."

"Did they find you before dark?"

"No, the raven did."

"The raven?"

"He came flying down off the top of the mountain

and he landed in this knobby old dead pine tree close by, and he just perched there staring at me. I was scared, at first. I thought he was waiting for me to die so he could eat me. You know, like vultures in an old western."

He stood up suddenly, found a piece of dead wood and broke it over his knee. He tossed the two pieces down toward the spring.

"He didn't eat you."

"Nope. After a while he flew over to another tree and perched again. I followed him. It was like something told me to go after him, even though I was still afraid of him. He was so black and big and mean-looking. But he hardly had to flap his wings to move from tree to tree, just sort of drifted through the air like . . ."

"Like what?" she prompted him when he stopped.

"Like some kind of black spirit, only not black in a bad sense, just natural and strong. After a while it suddenly hit me, he's beautiful." He picked up another piece of wood and threw it in a high arc down the trail. "So I followed him every time he flew off. I was scared to death he'd fly away where I wouldn't be able to find him, but he never did, he always landed close. So I followed him right out of the woods onto this trail, to where we are now. I saw the shelter and the trail and I knew I'd be okay, and when I looked up he was gone. Just disappeared into the shadows."

He turned to face her, grinning nervously in case she was laughing at him, but she wasn't laughing. "I loved that raven for saving me. I didn't even know he was a raven until later when I put it together that he was different from a crow. But I loved him. It was the first time I ever loved anything outside, you know. Outside the family."

"Did you stay at the shelter for the night?"

"I had sense enough to keep to the trail going down and met a search party coming up just after dark. My father was bullshit. My mother cried a lot. John was disappointed."

Matt laughed. He wiped the sweat off his forehead with his sleeve. Andrea was watching him closely. "Just a crazy kid story."

"You didn't tell your parents about it?"

"They never really gave me a chance to. And besides, I didn't want to tell anyone."

"But you've told me."

"Yeah." He walked over to where his backpack lay on its side on the floor of the shelter, and struggled into the straps. "Well, I thought you might . . ." He hesitated. "I was just a dumb kid and probably that raven was wondering what the hell I was doing there on *his* mountain. He just happened to . . . I mean, if you circle a mountain long enough, you're bound to come across a trail."

She stood up. "You don't have to apologize for thinking it was magic."

He looked at her. "No, I guess I don't."

She pulled the strap from her canvas bag up higher on her shoulder.

"I come up here sometimes," he told her. "Looking for ravens, wondering, when I do spot some, if one of them might be the same one, from back then. Doesn't make much sense now. I mean, there's no way I could know if it was." He shrugged. "But I like to see them."

She looked up toward the dome of the mountain, hidden behind the trees. "Let's go all the way to the top," she said.

When they reached open ledges again, they could see the top of the mountain about a quarter of a mile farther on. They raced over the flat ledges, with the enormous view on either side, hills beyond counting marching away on both sides toward horizons lost in the farthest blue haze.

Below the final dome the trail led around to the left. Matt waved Andrea in that direction, then started straight up the rock face.

"Matt!"

"Go on. I'll meet you at the top." He pulled himself up onto a narrow ledge, searched ahead for the next handhold above him.

"It's too steep," she shouted up to him. "Come down."

He ignored her. As he climbed higher, the wind began to snap at his backpack, trying to blow him off the face. He held himself close against the rock, not daring to look down to see if she were still watching or had taken the trail to the left. He was more frightened than he wanted her to see. He kept his gaze on the wrinkles in the rock above him.

"Matt!" Her voice sounded tiny already, blowing away on the wind that swept across the face of Firetop's final summit. He wedged his foot into a crack and chanced a quick look down. He couldn't see her.

He was halfway up before he realized that the handholds were petering out, smoothing into the rock. He did not think he could go back, for that one look down had really unnerved him. His hands groped above his head, searching for a purchase on the rock face. The tips of his fingers slipped over a narrow imperfection in the rock. He was getting tired; he couldn't stay forever hanging there. He lunged up toward the one tiny hold above him.

His fingers caught on it and held, but his right foot came free below. For a long second he hung there by one hand, his left boot still pressing down on an inch of ledge. Then his other hand found a grip above the first and he was able to shift his weight over onto a small knob of granite to his right. From there the way led more easily up at a slant to the top.

Strong hands gripped his shoulders as he wriggled over the edge. He pulled himself down into the summit bowl and rolled over onto his back as far as his backpack would permit him. Above him the sky loomed endlessly blue.

"You ass," Andrea said. Her face, white and glistening with sweat, swung down toward him. "You jerk, you fool, you imbecile."

He laughed. He couldn't stop himself, she looked so funny upside down above him, he felt so joyously returned to safety. The wind blew her hair across the blue, blue sky. He reached up and tried to catch it, tried to smooth it down against her face. She grabbed his hand.

"Are you happy now?" she asked angrily. "Did you prove something?"

He nodded. "Yes, I did."

# Chapter 12

*T*hey ate their lunch there in the summit bowl with the wind snatching at their hair and the view stretching off for miles and miles in all directions: ridge line following ridge line toward the far horizons like deep, green waves. They huddled together to keep out of the cold, wrapped in two extra shirts he had brought in his backpack.

Andrea was much taken with the view of Lake Craddock below them to the southeast. "It looks like a puddle," she said.

He glanced at her, then went back to tearing pieces off the loaf of bread she had brought.

"No, really. Like you could reach down and pick it up in one hand."

He pointed beyond the lake. "There's Bredstone, and that column of smoke is from the foundry in Ellington." As he continued to point out landmarks in an arc around them, she turned to smile at him.

"This is another of your favorite places."

He nodded. "Last winter I came up before the snow got deep, and the air was so clear it was like looking at a contour map. I mean, you could see everything in three states."

"Did you come alone?"

"Yeah. I can't get anyone around here interested in hiking Firetop." And his mother had been furious when she found out.

He looked down at the bread in his lap. He handed her a piece.

"It must be cold up here in winter," she said.

He shrugged. "Sure, but it's worth it. I saw a big flock of snow buntings fly out of that valley over there, sweep across the top of the mountain, and settle down by that little pocket of grass. Must have been a hundred of them. That's not something you're going to see in town."

She looked at him over her cup of water, a smile tugging at her mouth. "No, it's not."

"You're laughing at me."

She shook her head. "No, I'm laughing at everyone else. I think I'm always going to like picturing you up here in the winter all bundled up and by yourself, with birds to keep you company."

Again he had the impression she was several years older than he was. "You're twenty," he said.

"What?"

"I'm still guessing your age. You're twenty."

She shook her head.

"Trouble is, I've forgotten my other guesses."

"Does it matter how old I am?"

He shrugged.

"People aren't one age. They shift around a lot."

He knew she was right, yet he persisted. "Are you in college?"

"I'll go, eventually." She dug into her canvas bag and brought out two apples and a candy bar. "Why the questions now?"

"I suddenly realized that summer is racing by and you'll be leaving soon."

"Well," she said. She polished the apples on her shirt and handed him one. "Summer isn't over yet."

In the early afternoon they started down. They stopped at the spring below the shelter to fill the canteen. Now that they were out of the wind, he wondered how he could convince her to stay on the mountain for the rest of the afternoon. He didn't want to go down.

He went to the shelter and pulled at a section of the metal roof. "The wind's going to take this away next winter." He looked around at the battered trees that crowded close by the building. "They don't protect it much."

She came up to join him and sat on the edge of the floor by the open side of the shelter. "It's lovely here."

She did not seem in any hurry to leave. He sat down beside her. A dozen things crowded to his tongue to say, but he did not manage to say any of them. What he finally said was, "Let's not go down yet. It's early. We can . . ."

As she shifted on the floor to face him, his voice trailed off into silence. He leaned forward to kiss her before she could speak. He caught her lips open against his own. As she began to pull back, he lost his balance and they fell together onto the soft, damp floor.

"Nice move," she said against his ear.

He kissed her again. This time she put her fingers around the back of his neck. But when she moved her face away, her eyes were looking outside, to the trees, the three-story boulder, the mountain path.

"I don't know, Matt," she said.

"No one's here," he told her. "No one's on the mountain except us. We can hear if anyone comes, we can . . ."

He felt her chest move against his when she laughed. "That's not what I'm wondering about, dummy," she said. She squirmed up into a sitting position. Seeing the expression on his face, she said, "Oh God, look at you." She turned away. "Look at you, looking at me that way."

Then she stood up and retrieved her canvas bag, which had fallen beside her. "Give me a minute," she said, and disappeared around the back of the shelter.


As the sun dropped behind the dome of Firetop, the little grove around the shelter filled with blue shadows. They pooled in the recesses beneath the branches of the trees, then spilled out at last to join the shadow moving up from the three-story boulder. This high up, changes in the light were slow to come, filtering down indirectly into the grove. Matt watched bits of the sky turn from blue to bronze.

"Did you really have a lover who was part of the French government?" he asked her.

She shifted her head on his chest but did not sit up. "What?"

"You told me you had a lover in Paris."

"Oh, Robbie. You don't want to know about him."

"Did he really work for the government?"

"His father was a diplomat. He . . ." She laughed softly. "I'm sorry I lied to you. You were just being such a little snot about my life." She said something else — in French, he thought. She laughed again. "But I shouldn't have lied."

"So what was Robbie like?"

She sat up. "Why is it that as soon as a boy's made love to you, he thinks your whole life is his to root around in?"

It was too late to call back his questions. "I was just curious because I thought he was older."

"Well, he was my age." She reached for her shirt. "It wasn't much. We . . . ran away together."

"What happened?"

"What do you mean, what happened?"

"You're not there now."

She sighed. "Nothing happened. When it wasn't fun anymore I . . ." She began pulling on her jeans. "I went back to my father."

He watched her finish dressing. He was afraid he had spoiled things. "I'll tell you anything you want to know about me."

"Anything?"

She was smiling. He nodded happily.

"You already told me something really special this morning," she said.

"We'd better go," Andrea said at last. "Daddy will be getting upset, wondering where I've wandered off to."

"Why do you stay with him?" he asked as he retrieved his boots. "You're old enough to be on your own."

At first he thought she wasn't going to answer. But beside the spring she paused to pull back her hair. "We must be a puzzle to you," she said.

"Yeah, you are."

Her eyes seemed part of the luminous evening under the trees. "We're special, he and I. After my mother left I kind of took her place. I don't mean in any kinky way. Just running the household and seeing to things, so he could be free to work on his writing. I was the one who helped him through the bad time when he knew he was going blind."

She said it proudly, as if no other person could have done what she had done. She led the way out onto the last shoulder of rocks above the ladder of tree roots.

"And that's why you stay with him, because you're his eyes?" he asked.

"Something like that."

"How long has he been blind?"

"Too long," she said. "Or not long enough. I don't know which." She looked down at the trail below. "But we still have good times. We travel. We entertain his friends. We..."

"What about *your* friends?"

She shrugged. "I've ... I've always known people older than I am. It was part of the way things were, all the time." She looked at him. "Except Robbie. And you."

Tears were beginning to trickle down her face. He wasn't sure he knew why she was crying, except that everything she was telling him sounded very sad.

He went ahead of her down the steep place, watching her footing above him.

"I guess I'm a very loyal person," she said. She joined him on the path below the tree roots. They stood very close. "Maybe because my mother never was."

They plunged down into the hardwood forest where darkness was already creeping up the hillside toward them.

"So you see," her voice came back to him through the still and chilly air, "I can't just say 'It's been swell, Daddy,' and walk away. After Mom left us, it was just him and me, for so long it's been just him and me." She waited for Matt to catch up where the path widened, and took his hand. "So I can't just desert him now. Can you see that?"

"Sure." He nodded. "Sure, I can see that."

In the dim light her face was a shadow, but he saw her hair fall loose again as she shook her head. "I've had a good life."

"Sounds like," he said. He fought to keep any trace of sarcasm out of his voice. He knew she was lying, more to herself than to him, but he had no desire to point this out to her.

"I've really had a wonderful time growing up," she said. "I was a very happy child."

# Chapter 13

*T*he next morning Matt ate breakfast with Andrea at the boathouse and then walked his bike out to the road. John was still asleep when he got to the house. Matt collected the tools he needed from the garage and put the ladder up against the sunny side of the house. He began scraping the old paint off the clapboards beside John's bedroom window. Whenever he found a loose clapboard, he renailed it.

"You're up early."

Matt looked over and saw John's face through the haze of his window screen.

"Well, it's a big house." Matt expected John to yell at him for waking him up, and he was ready with a sharp reply.

"Be out as soon as I have a cup of coffee," John said, and disappeared from the window.

Half an hour later John was below him on the smaller ladder, scraping diligently with the other scraper, a cigarette drooping out of one corner of his mouth.

"Since when are you smoking?" Matt asked.

"Since this summer."

"Well, won't Mom and Dad be proud of us. We've developed all kinds of bad habits while they've been away."

John nailed a loose clapboard under one of the kitchen windows. "I won't ask you what your bad habit is." He blew out a cloud of blue smoke.

Matt climbed down to move his ladder. They looked at each other in the glare of sunlight off the wall.

"When are you going to get the dent in the car fixed?"

John shrugged. "When I get around to it."

"What if Mrs. Gannon sees it?" Matt studied his brother's face. "Mom's calling her, too, you know."

"I'll take care of it."

"I'm not lending you the money to pay for it if you're broke," Matt said, still probing.

"Go back up your ladder," John told him, but he didn't raise his voice.

The telephone rang just before eleven o'clock. While John ran in to answer it, Matt shifted both ladders to the front of the house. John leaned out the front door.

"It's Mom. She wants *you*."

Matt knew he had missed too many calls. He was going to have to think up a good excuse. He hurried into the house.

"Matt?" His mother's voice was hidden behind a loud crackle. "Is that you?"

"Sure is."

"I can barely hear you."

"Must be a bad connection. Where are you calling from?"

"Naples."

"Having fun? How's Dad?"

"He's fine, dear."

He had to guess at her words, the noise on the line was so loud.

"Why are you never home when we call?"

"Bad timing, I guess."

"What's this . . ." The rest of her question disappeared into the static.

"What?"

"John said you've been keeping company with some summer girl." Even through the static he could hear the distaste in her voice.

That jerk, Matt thought. Aloud he said, "Yeah."

"What?"

"I said, yes, I am."

"You are what?"

Matt shouted into the phone. "Spending time with a girl!"

"Don't shout! It makes it worse."

"Sorry."

"Well, who is she?"

"A girl."

"Matt!"

"Well, you don't know her. What can I tell you?"

"Is she nice?"

That word again. So this was where he had picked it up. Aloud he said, "She's fun." He wondered if his mother

134

would be happier if he had developed a crush on Old Man Smitty, the janitor at school.

After a long pause she said, "Well, be careful."

"Of what?" he asked, but either his mother didn't hear his question or she chose to ignore it.

"Are you and John getting along?"

"Sure." He didn't tell her that they got along by putting the whole town between them.

"Your father and I will be home the twenty-fifth. We'll either fly up to Ellington or you can meet us at the airport in Boston. We'll call you before our flight."

"Okay."

"Good-bye, Matt."

"Good-bye." He did not hear her hang up. "Good-bye," he said again.

"Love you," she said.

He knew she wouldn't hang up until he said it. "Love you too, Mom," he mumbled.

On his way out of the house he went through the kitchen and glanced at the calendar. Out front he picked up his scraper where he had dropped it on the lawn.

"We have a little more than a week to get this house painted," he said. "They're coming home the twenty-fifth."

Up on his ladder, John bore down hard on a rough place in the trim around one window. "We'll make it."

"Have to work all day every day."

"So, we'll work all day every day."

Matt shifted his ladder a foot to the right and climbed up. "Why did you tell her about Andrea?"

"Who?"

"The girl I've been seeing."

John looked up at him, squinting his eyes through the smoke of another cigarette. "I had to tell her something. I figured she'd be relieved you weren't doing something worse, like partying with the crowd up at Point Rollins." He pulled the cigarette from his lips. "Why? Does it bother her?"

"Seems to." Matt reached into his shirt pocket for a nail. "What did you tell her?"

"Oh, hell!" John said, flicking his cigarette down onto the lawn. "I told her you had the hots for some summer girl and I hardly ever saw you anymore."

"Nicely put."

"What the hell was I supposed to say?" John shouted. He threw a handful of nails up at Matt. They bounced off his back. "Stay home and talk to her yourself."

"I'm not coming home."

"I'm not asking you to." John lit another cigarette. "Just shut up. You're giving me a headache."

They worked the rest of the morning in silence. During their break for lunch, John drove off in the car. Matt tackled the west side of the house alone. The sun was hot and yesterday's breeze had died out during the night. He took off his shirt and tied a handkerchief around his head to keep the sweat out of his eyes.

John was gone for hours. When he came back, he leaned on the car horn all the way up the street, then pulled into the driveway at such a speed that he had to slam on the brakes to avoid running into the garage. Matt paused from his scraping to listen to the skid. When there was no crash, he went back to work.

"Hello, little Matty."

Matt looked down. John was coming around the front of the house, a can of beer in his hand.

"Glad you could make it," Matt told him.

John shook the ladder he was standing on. "Better be nice or I'll knock this ladder right out from under you."

Matt went back to his scraping.

"Scared?" John taunted.

Matt shook his head. "Not of you."

John gave the ladder a kick and went into the house. Matt took a deep breath. He was holding onto the ladder so tightly with his free hand that his knuckles were white.

He had moved the ladders around to the back before John appeared again.

"It's after five," he said. "Don't you ever quit?"

Matt ignored him.

"Okay, okay, where the hell's my scraper?"

Matt pointed to the side yard. John went after the scraper and joined him at the back of the house. The sun was hanging low in the sky by the time they finished the last strips of clapboard.

"Okay," John said. "We putty the windows tomorrow, then start on the trim."

Matt nodded. As he walked toward his bike, John called to him.

He stopped. "What?"

John seemed unsure of what he wanted to say. "You can move back, you know. It's your house too."

Matt looked at him. First his brother threatened to pull the ladder out from under him, then a couple hours later he was inviting him to come home.

"Well, whatever," John said.

"Sometime," Matt answered at last.

The next day they worked on the windows, replacing the putty wherever it had fallen out. It was slow, monotonous work, but Matt liked the smell of the glazing compound.

John went in and got them both beers just before lunch. "Sorry about yesterday," he said as he handed Matt his.

Matt couldn't remember his brother ever apologizing for anything before. He didn't know what to say.

"Frame it," John said with a sour look on his face. "That's the last sorry you'll ever get from me."

They went back to work. From time to time Matt glanced at John, wondering what was going on. They worked all day, progressing around the house, this time from window to window. Toward sundown John got into the car without a word and drove off. Matt finished the last window and then went into the garage to clean the glazing compound off his hands.

The house seemed lonely and deserted when no one was there. He glanced down the empty driveway. Did John feel it too, when he was here alone?

He rode his bike back to the boathouse, eager to see Andrea. While he waited for her he sat on the edge of the deck with his legs in the water. He could do this now with only a little fear. He thought that he should still be trying to go in deeper, but he really didn't want to get involved again in that daily torture. Andrea didn't bully him anymore about it. He had managed to wade in up to his waist; he couldn't find the courage to force himself to float. You could call it a partial victory. Or a partial defeat. It depended on how . . .

Someone was coming down through the grass. He looked up, expecting to see Andrea with his supper. Instead he saw her father.

He had only seen Stark Stafford once before, back on the day his parents left for Europe, when John had blocked the one-way street, forcing Andrea to back up the Mercedes. But he had seen photographs, like the one on the back cover of *Sound Side*. He recognized him from the man's thick white hair and from the way he was swinging his thin cane before him as he came down the hill.

Matt watched him come closer, wondering if Mr. Stafford knew where he was. Was he aiming for the boathouse? Did he even know that he was walking toward water? He walked with his head tilted back, as if he were afraid that if he did walk into something, it would be his face that would be injured. He was dressed in a sweat shirt and white pants. The sweat shirt was so big his thin upper body seemed lost within it.

There was a scowl on his face. His lips were moving, as if he were counting to himself. When he suddenly stopped, the cane continued to swing through a tight arc in front of his legs.

They looked at each other, or rather, Matt looked and Stark Stafford listened, across the twenty or thirty feet that separated them. Matt wanted to say hello, but he couldn't.

They stayed that way for at least a minute, though it felt like much longer. It was Andrea who broke the spell, as she came running down from the house.

Her father heard her and turned around. She said something too low for Matt to understand, then began leading her father back up the hill toward the house. Matt had not moved from where he sat on the deck.

Andrea looked once at him over her shoulder, but she did not say a word to him.

When she came down later she was quiet and subdued. She went for a swim, and he stood leaning against the boathouse, watching her. He had her towel ready when she came out. Later, he could smell the lake water in her hair as he held her, as she shivered in the chill air.

"I can't come down tomorrow night," she told him a little later as she was getting ready to leave. "Can you eat at home after you're done painting?"

"Sure. No problem. I shouldn't be . . ."

"I'm glad to bring you down your supper," she said quickly. "It's just that tomorrow night I can't."

"What's happening tomorrow night?" he asked as he followed her to the edge of the field. "Will I see you at all?"

"I'm afraid not. We're having a party for some of our friends from Boston. We haven't seen them all summer."

"Couldn't I come?" he asked, and then was angry with himself.

"You wouldn't enjoy yourself."

"How do you know?"

"You just wouldn't," she said. "These people are . . ."

"What?"

"You'd find them boring."

"Do you?"

She ignored his question. "Come on, kiss me, I've got to go up."

"You don't want me to meet your father."

"That's not true."

"Then what's the matter?" He tried to suppress the next question, but it came out anyway. "Are you ashamed of me?"

She sighed. He did not like the sound of it. "I'm not ashamed of you," she said. "That's really dumb."

He was not convinced. "I think you are."

She turned and walked away, no longer waiting for his good-night kiss. "The party's at eight," she called back over her shoulder. "Come if you want."

# Chapter 14

*H*ad her parting words not seemed to him to be a challenge, he would not have gone to the party. He would have allowed himself to use any of the dozen reasons for not going that occurred to him the next day while he painted with John. He would have stayed quietly down at the boathouse by himself.

But he felt she had slapped him in the face when she walked away, tossing her unenthusiastic invitation over her shoulder. If she thought he didn't dare come to the party, he would show her that he did. If she thought he was too much of a social misfit to be trusted in the company of strangers, he would show her that he could rise to the occasion despite his shyness and do just fine.

He would be as sophisticated as any of her Boston friends.

He and John were now putting on the first coat of white paint. The trim was all done and they were slapping paint onto the clapboards. Or rather, John was slapping on the paint and Matt was brushing it on carefully.

"You're the world's slowest painter," John shouted to him late in the afternoon.

"Yeah, but the best."

When they were done for the day, Matt took a shower and put on his best pair of cords, a new turtleneck, his dressiest jacket. He stood playing with his hair for ten minutes in front of his bedroom mirror. When at last he went downstairs, John was frying hamburgers in the iron skillet on the stove.

"Want a couple?"

Matt shook his head. He didn't dare eat; his stomach was already doing flops. John turned from the stove and saw him.

"Don't say anything, okay?" Matt pleaded. "Just drive me and my bike over to the barrens so I don't get all sweated up."

John raised his eyebrows. "I'm not supposed to tease you?"

"Right."

"That's asking a lot, you know."

Matt didn't have anything clever to say. He waited in the living room while John ate his supper. He flipped through the pages of a magazine, but the pictures were only splashes of color to his eyes.

They jammed his bike into the car trunk and drove slowly toward the lake. Already some of the cottages were vacant. The cool nights now signaled the end of summer, and the slow drift of people away from the lake conveyed a sense of the emptiness to come.

As they drove by the town beach, Matt saw Michele

getting out of an open jeep with a boy he'd never seen before.

"Who's that?"

"Michele."

"I know it's Michele. Who's she with?" He watched Michele turn around as they drove past. She grabbed the boy's hand and pulled him toward the water. "I thought you and her . . ."

"Let it alone." John stepped down hard on the gas.

"Did you have a fight?"

"I said, drop it!"

"Okay, okay." Matt glanced at his brother.

"What's the matter?" John demanded.

"Nothing." Matt wiped his hands on the knees of his pants. "Nothing, I guess."

At the edge of the pine barrens John stopped the car. "Have fun. And for Christ's sake, stop looking so scared."

Matt got out and pulled his bike from the trunk. As he wheeled it off the road, he heard John turn the car around and drive back toward town.

He waited at the boathouse as darkness crept in beneath the ridge. Eventually he could see lights glowing in every downstairs window in the Staffords' house. When he walked up the hill, his heart was going much too fast; he knew his hands would remain sweaty no matter how many times he wiped them on his pants.

The drive was crowded with cars, most of them foreign, most of them new. The front door was open; he could hear music floating out from the stereo. He knocked a couple of times. When no one came, he opened the screen door and slipped inside.

He saw his face in the mirror above the table in the front hall. Trying to smile, he walked on, through the hall and into the dining room.

The dining room table had been transformed into a buffet, with platters of hors d'oeuvres, bowls of crackers, stoneware jugs of dips and relishes. The centerpiece was a crystal punch bowl piled high with sliced fruit: watermelon, cantaloupe, honeydew, garnished with strawberries.

Every car outside must have arrived full of people, because every corner of the house was full.

The babble was deafening. Almost no one saw him come in. A few people standing by the bar that had been set up near the sideboard turned in his direction, but that was only because he tripped over the threshold as he came into the room and nearly fell into their arms. He nodded, perhaps he even managed to smile. They turned away.

He went into the front room, looking for Andrea, cutting through the crowd around the couch, thinking he had spotted her near the stereo, realizing just in time that this was someone whose hair, from behind, vaguely resembled Andrea's. Turning, he saw her cross the dining room, a platter of food balanced in one hand, a drink in the other.

She was dressed in a long, swirling skirt of browns, reds, and blacks. Her brilliant white blouse looked like silk.

He fought his way back through the crowd. She saw him as she swung the tray down onto the table. But before he could break out of the front room, she waved and disappeared into the kitchen. He continued after her and found her there, at last, with three stout women in ruffled white aprons.

The women were preparing a large salad. Andrea

watched them closely, making suggestions every few seconds. They looked down at their work and tried to ignore her.

"Hi," she said as he came up beside her. "Just get here?"

He nodded.

She touched his arm, straightened his jacket. "You look sexy."

"You look sexier."

She smiled. Her face was flushed, her large eyes glistened with excitement. "I love parties." She handed him a glass of wine and pushed him toward the door. "Go on out and mingle. There are some famous people out there."

"I don't know a soul."

"Introduce yourself. Really, all they want to do is talk about themselves anyway."

He allowed himself to be pushed out into the dining room. When he turned to say something more to Andrea, she was already back at the table where the three stout women were chopping celery and green peppers. "We've got to begin on the chicken," she told them.

He faced the crowd. Everyone was talking, no one was listening, no one looked his way. For a horrible moment he thought he was going to run from the room. Then someone grabbed his hand and shook it.

"My God, you must be Carlton's boy!"

Matt saw a large, red-faced man smiling at him expectantly. "No, I'm . . ."

"Hardly recognized you, you've grown so."

Matt shook his head. "I'm Matt Zaharis," he said, but the red-faced man had already turned away.

It was a while before he realized not a single guest at the party was under forty. Many were in their sixties and seventies. Matt wondered what Andrea could possibly find to say to them.

But she was the darling of the crowd tonight. Every time she tore herself away from the kitchen, she was surrounded by people who wanted to talk with her. He could not get near her again, and after a while he stopped trying.

Sometimes he noticed her glancing his way, more often with a frown on her face as the evening dragged on. Once she pointed over the heads of the couple she was talking to, toward the front room. Later, she swept by him, her skirt brushing against his legs.

"Mix," she told him in a low voice as she went by. "Don't just stand there like a lump."

He tried. He found a woman standing by the row of windows that faced the lake, and, encouraged by the fact that she was alone too, he said, "It's a nice view."

That word again . . .

"It's a lovely view," he tried. "Great view." He looked down into his empty wine glass as if expecting to find inspiration there. "I like the view, don't you?"

When the woman looked at him as if he had dropped suddenly out of a cobweb, he felt himself losing control. "Are you a lump?" he heard himself ask her. "Andrea thinks I'm a lump. Are you one too?"

"I beg your pardon."

"That's all right. Lumps have to stick together. Can I get you another drink?"

She shook her head, backing away from him toward a

group of men near the buffet. Perhaps one of them was her husband, her escort, her *father* . . . He didn't pursue her. Flushed with success, he looked around for new fields to conquer.

In the wide doorway between the two rooms, Andrea's father was talking to a group of women gathered about him in an adoring circle. As he spoke to them he waved his cane over his head as if it were a magic wand with which he hoped to change them all into wood nymphs. Matt decided to go over and introduce himself. After all, it was time they said hello . . .

But before he could reach the far side of the room, the bartender called to him.

"Hey, kid."

Matt stopped to look at him.

"Yeah, you."

Matt walked to the bar and set down his empty glass. The bartender was a sunburned blond with a peeling nose and big shoulders. "How about helping out for a minute while I take a break?"

"Me?"

The bartender nodded. "I just want to duck out and smoke a joint. Won't be five minutes."

Matt looked down at the array of bottles. "I don't know. I . . ."

"Nothing to it. Nobody's drinking anything exotic. You ever mix drinks before?"

"A couple of times."

"Then you're a cinch for the job." The bartender untied his apron and held it out to Matt. "Put this on. It'll make you look official."

Red letters across the front of the apron said, Name Your Poison. While Matt stood there hesitating, the bartender draped the apron over his head and quickly went around to tie it in back. "Here," he said, taking a yachting cap from a box behind the bar. "Put this on. Adds a touch of class."

The cap was too big. It slid off to one side of his head and came to rest against his ear. "I look like a jerk," Matt said.

The bartender shook his head. "You look great. Really, kid. Be right back." And before Matt could say anything more, he slipped away through the crowd.

Matt took his place behind the bar. Except in a liquor store, he had never seen so much to drink all gathered together, much less had any responsibility for its proper dispensing. But there was a certain relief in having something concrete to do. He found a gallon jug of white wine and refilled his own glass. He took a sip. Nothing to it.

"Scotch on the rocks."

Matt looked up at the red-faced man who had mistaken him for someone else earlier. There was no hint of recognition in the man's bloodshot eyes now.

"Scotch on the rocks, yes sir." Matt looked over the rows of bottles.

"Johnnie Walker Red," the man prompted him.

Matt found the bottle and dropped a handful of ice in the man's glass. He filled it the rest of the way with Scotch.

The man laughed. "Trying to get me plowed?"

Matt shrugged. "It'll save you a trip."

The man looked at him closely. "Where's the other kid?"

"On his break."

"You're kind of young, aren't you?"

Matt shook his head. "I just look young. Actually, I'm thirty-two."

A group of people all asked for wine. He had no problem finding what they wanted. He was beginning to enjoy himself. He retied the apron and stood there smiling, waiting for more orders.

"Is there any of the champagne left?"

He looked behind him, found a low tub of ice with one bottle of champagne still in it. He held the bottle up to the woman who had requested it.

She nodded. "That's the stuff, sonny."

He was hoping she might just take the bottle with her, but she stood there instead with her empty glass in her hand, waiting for him to fill it.

"There's little wires and things," she said when she realized, finally, that he was looking for a corkscrew. "You got to untwist them, you know?" She smiled. "Hey, are you a real bartender or just a mascot?"

"I'm real," he told her, straightening the yachting cap. He tore off the foil from the neck of the bottle and began untwisting the wires around the cork. They came off easily enough, but the cork itself was wedged tightly into the neck of the bottle.

"Twist it around," the woman told him.

As he worked on it, she shook her head. "You're being too rough. You're going to have a mess on your hands."

He didn't know what she was talking about until the cork popped through his fingers, flying out across the room into the crowd. Someone screamed, several other people laughed. He was busy trying to keep the foaming champagne from spilling out all over the bar.

"Save me some, save me some!" the woman squealed. She pushed her glass under the foaming wine. When her glass was full, Matt tipped up the bottle with what little remained of the champagne and searched for a rag to clean up the spill.

"What do you think you're doing now?"

He looked up and saw Andrea standing there glaring at him.

"Helping out," he told her.

"I can see that."

"Well, the bartender wanted a break."

"So you just volunteered to take his place."

He tried to meet her eyes. "No, he asked me."

She pushed angrily at her hair. "Take that stupid apron off and get out from behind there." She snatched the yachting cap off his head.

"What's wrong with the apron?" He looked down at it, smoothing away a few drops of champagne. "It's kind of clever." He looked up. "It's me, don't you think?"

But she had already turned away. He watched her push through the crowd. She hadn't laughed at any of his jokes. She hadn't even smiled.

When the real bartender came back a couple minutes later, he was shaking his head. "What did you do, kid? That's one wound-up lady."

"Nothing." Matt took off the apron and handed it back

to him. "I mean, I did fine." He pointed to the tub of ice. "You're out of champagne."

The bartender laughed for no particular reason. "That chick has a streak of bitch in her a yard wide." He finished cleaning up the spilled champagne. "Well, she'll cool down." As Matt started to drift away, he looked up and found Matt's glass. "What were you drinking? Chablis?"

"Yeah, I guess."

The bartender laughed again. "Here, I'll fix you a real drink." He took a large glass and began pouring into it from several bottles. Matt stared in amazement as the different-colored liquors stayed each on its own level, resulting in a drink that was a series of colored rings all the way up the glass. The bartender stuck in a straw.

"Handle with care," he said as he handed Matt the glass. "It's dynamite."

Matt took his drink into the front room. It would be a good idea to avoid Andrea until she had a chance to get over her bad temper. He found a perch for himself on the stairs, where he could watch the crowd without having to be part of it. He would wait for most of the guests to leave, then go find Andrea and apologize.

The drink tasted good but burned his throat going down. It felt warm once it made it all the way to his stomach. He sipped it through the straw, trying not to destroy the layers until he had to.

Andrea's father was on the couch talking with a small, wizened man barely half his size. They seemed to be the best of friends, laughing together over everything Mr. Stafford said. Matt watched their mouths, unable, through all the noise of the party, to make out a word they were say-

152

ing. He did not think they even knew he was sitting there, in the shadows on the stairs, watching.

He would have been content to stay there, watching Stark Stafford, listening to the music blaring from the speakers against the wall, but he started to feel sick to his stomach and went upstairs, looking for a bathroom.

The upstairs hall was dark except for a small lamp at one end. He found the bathroom just in time and lost the lovely striped drink along with everything else he had consumed during the evening. But he was drunk enough so that he didn't feel bad afterward, only tired and sleepy in a sad, peaceful way. Instead of going back down to the party, he wandered along the hall until he found Andrea's room.

He had no business there, he knew, but he went in and turned on the light beside her bed. She had taken the pencil sketch she had done of him at the boathouse and tacked it up on one wall. When he saw it there he felt a stab of guilt.

He was sorry he had made her so angry tonight. He was sorry he was such a disappointment . . . He touched the blue spread on her bed, he touched her pillow. On her bureau he found one of her bottles of perfume and opened it and sniffed it.

There were books in a pile on her night table that he longed to flip through, just to see what she liked to read. There was a large notebook there, too, that might be her diary. He knew he could never violate her privacy and look inside it, any more than he could open her bureau drawers and go through her clothes.

But for a moment, as he stood there, he felt an almost

overpowering need to do these things, to know her more than he knew her now, to find real intimacy in the private things of her private life.

Steps in the hallway broke into his thoughts. He turned toward the door; it was too late to escape. But it wasn't Andrea who discovered him there, it was her father.

Matt took a deep breath. "I suppose you're wondering what I'm doing in your daughter's room," he began. "Actually, I'm very fond of your daughter, but I know I . . ." He went on and on; it wouldn't stop, this flow of words, as he tried to explain away his presence there in Andrea's room. Stark Stafford stood in the doorway, swaying slightly, his cane beside his right leg, and then, suddenly, he brought up the cane and slapped it against Matt's face.

"Get out of here," he said in a low, hoarse voice. "Get out of my house *now*."

Pain made Matt's eyes water. He reached up and touched the welt on his cheek. As he ran for the door, Stark Stafford stepped back to let him go through. He did not flail out with the cane again. He didn't need to.

Matt ran down the stairs, knowing he would have to run all the way through the party to find his way out. He held one hand to his cheek to hide the burning slash mark Andrea's father had put there with his cane, but he knew it did no good. He felt everyone staring at him as he ran for the front door, felt sure they could see the livid mark on his face and read it like an ugly word.

# Chapter 15

"*I* told you you wouldn't enjoy the party," Andrea said to him the following night at the boathouse. She sat at the edge of the deck, dangling her legs in the water. "I told you you'd hate it."

"Yeah, you did." He had told her that the bruise on his cheek came from a fall off the ladder while painting. She did not know of his encounter with her father in her room.

"You might at least have come around to say good-night to me before you left."

He nodded now, sticking with his pose. "I should have. I couldn't find you."

She pulled her legs up onto the deck and turned to peer at him through the dusk light. "You could have found me if you'd wanted to. You just wanted to storm off in a huff because you hated everyone there."

"Maybe something like that," he mumbled, more to himself than to her.

"You could have tried a little harder. How do you expect people to like you if you don't like them? Do you blame them if they think you're . . . you're weird or something?"

"Did someone say that?"

She pulled back her hair in both hands and stared down at her knees. "People would like you if you'd give them a chance."

He did not want to meet her anger head-on. He wanted to deflect it if he could. "I did try," he said softly. "And I was really trying to help when I took over for the bartender."

She looked up. It was too dark now for him to read her expression. "I don't even want to talk about that," she said.

"Would you like me to move out of the boathouse?" he asked her.

"What?"

"Do you want me to get out of the boathouse?"

"Why?"

"I don't think your father would like it if he knew I was here."

"Did you . . ."

"I didn't say a word to him last night," he quickly lied. "I didn't go near him."

"Then why are you worried about it?"

"Just a hunch," he said.

"Do you want to move out?" she asked. Her voice was softer now; the anger, he hoped, had melted away with the scolding she'd given him.

"No, I want to stay."

She stood up and dove into the water. When she came up, she was far out into the lake. "I want you to stay," she called through the darkness between them. "Okay?"

"Okay," he said.

The next morning he and John began putting on the second coat of white. The first coat had finished drying yesterday.

By five o'clock in the afternoon they could see their way to the end of the job. After moving the ladders for the next day, they did a slow circle around the house, beer cans in their hands, surveying their work.

"Not bad for one man and a dub," John said.

Matt had to agree with him that they were doing a good job. Except for the quantity of paint that now decorated the lawn and shrubs near the house, the whole thing looked professionally done.

"When you flunk out of college," he told John, "you've got a trade to fall back on."

"Thanks." John drained his beer and crumpled the can. "And you can quit school and come work for me. I'll pay you what you're worth, ten cents an hour." John threw his beer can toward the pile in the garage. "If we push as hard tomorrow we can finish the second coat. Then all we'll have left to do is touch up the trim where you've messed it over."

"And clean up the house where you've been living like a slob since I left."

"Yeah." John looked at the paint on his hands. "Why don't you move back?"

Matt laughed. "Just so I can clean it before they come home?"

"Well." John looked up at him, then away. "You could help me, at least."

"Maybe."

As Matt rode his bike back toward the lake, Mrs. Gannon hailed him from her flower garden. He spun up into her driveway.

"Your parents are coming home soon," she said.

"On the twenty-fifth."

She nodded. "Yes, I know." She seemed hesitant about saying what was on her mind. "You haven't been around the house much, except painting."

He waited to see what she was driving at.

"Your brother . . ." She ran her fingers over the blooms of a yellow rose bush. Petals fell to her feet, but she did not seem to notice. "I never approved of all the parties your brother threw for his noisy friends." She sighed. "But at least that was normal for someone his age."

Puzzled, Matt waited for her to go on. The setting sun was hitting him in the eyes. He squinted against the glare.

"Do you know, Matt, that he sits now every night on your front porch with the house all in darkness and no one ever comes and he never goes out? He just sits there in the dark, and sometimes he's still there when the light comes in the morning."

"No, I didn't know that."

"I didn't think you did." She looked down and suddenly discovered the damage she had done to the roses. "Oh dear."

"Thank you for telling me," Matt called softly as he turned his bike toward the street.

"I know you think I'm a nosy old gossip, Matthew, but . . ."

"We don't think that," Matt told her.

"It's only because I care about you boys. Seems as though you grew up here in my house, too."

"I know we did, Mrs. Gannon."

"John's not as sure of himself as he pretends to be," she told him as he rode away. "Sometimes the biggest mouths hide the biggest fears."

At the boathouse Matt lathered himself with soap and rinsed off with lake water that he scooped up in a tin can. He read a paperback novel until the light grew too dim, but if a quiz had been given on the book he was reading, he would have failed it miserably. His mind kept drifting away from the words on the page to thoughts of John, alone back at the house.

Matt had often considered himself an only child, despite the fact that he had a brother. In so many ways he had grown up alone. For the first time he realized that for John there may have existed this same solitude.

He sat in a chair inside the screened porch, looking out on the lake, watching the surface of the water fade from soft violet and pink to a gray shadow of the night itself. When he heard someone moving down through the field, he got up and went to the porch door, thinking it was Andrea.

"You there."

It was August Burns, the town constable.

Matt watched him walk toward the boathouse through the tall, brown grass. He had his full uniform on, and was even carrying his gun.

"Come on, boy, get your stuff together. You're leaving."

Matt opened the screen door and stepped out onto the deck. August Burns stopped at the edge of the field.

"I'll be damned!"

"I'm Matt Zaharis," Matt told him.

"I know who you are. I can see that now. Never expected it was you down here plaguing the old man."

"I'm not plaguing him. Andrea said I could stay here."

"Well, I don't know much about that." August Burns scratched his stubbly face. His thin legs looked bowed by the weight of his heavy uniform. "I'm here to see to it that you vacate these premises," he said, as if Matt were a tenant who was six months behind on his rent. "Mr. Stafford wants you out of here tonight."

"Did you talk to Andrea? She can tell you that . . ."

"It's Mr. Stafford owns this boathouse," August Burns interrupted him. "And it's Mr. Stafford wants you removed." The constable shook his head and continued more gently, "Now wouldn't your mother be ashamed to find out you was behaving this way."

Matt looked up at the house on the hill above them. In the falling dusk there was a light showing in the kitchen. Was Andrea watching through the window? Would she come down to put a stop to this?

"How about I go in the morning?" Matt suggested hopefully.

160

"How about you get your gear packed and ride on out of here." August Burns stepped up onto the deck. "Or do I got to put you in the lockup for the night?"

While the town constable waited there on the deck, Matt jammed everything into his backpack that he could put his hands on in the darkness inside the porch.

"Get it all, boy," August Burns told him, interrupting his own tuneless whistle. "You won't be coming back for seconds."

Matt searched out the last of his books, knocking over one of the porch chairs in his haste. A hot feeling of shame was spreading through him. He had never had anything but the friendliest of dealings with August Burns before this, and now the town constable was treating him like a criminal.

"I got it all," he said as he came out onto the deck.

"That's good," August Burns said. "That your ten-speed?"

"Yes, sir."

"Okay, then wheel it up that hill and get on home."

Matt pulled the straps of his backpack onto his shoulders. "I'll go out through the woods, if it's okay," he said softly. "I don't want . . ."

"You don't want what?"

I don't want Andrea to see me, he thought. To the constable he said, "It's easier to go out that way."

"Well then, get."

Matt wheeled his bike toward the barrens. August Burns walked after him, as if to make sure he didn't try to sneak back.

"What's with you Zaharis boys this summer, anyway?"
Matt stopped. "What do you mean?"

"You holed up here, your brother doing everything
he can to get himself killed." August Burns caught up
with him. He tapped Matt on the shoulder. "I'm pretty
damn sure it was your brother went off the Point Rollins
road and slammed up all them mailboxes. You tell him
to knock off the drinking or I'll bust him one of these
nights and he'll lose that license of his and your folks
will be real happy when they get home."

"I'll tell him," Matt said softly.

"You do that." August Burns slapped his arm. "Get
going. Don't be taking all night about it."

Before he reached the trees Matt thought he saw a
movement above him on the hillside and stopped to look,
but there was nothing astir in the field except a faint
wind that rippled over the grass.

August Burns still stood there, watching to make sure
he didn't come back. "Go on, boy."

A hundred yards into the woods, Matt stopped again
and waited five minutes, maybe longer. But Andrea did
not come after him.

At the house John heard him putting his bike away in
the garage. "That you, Matt?"

"Yeah."

On the dark front porch Matt tripped over a pile of
empty cans. "Jesus, John." He fumbled for the light.
They both squinted when it flashed on.

"How the hell can you sit here in the dark that way?"
Matt demanded.

John didn't even have his pants on. He was sitting in his underwear on the edge of a chair, an ashtray full of cigarette butts by his side. Matt counted a dozen empty beer cans on the floor.

"Jesus, John," he repeated.

But his brother was staring at his backpack. "You coming home?"

"Andrea's father had me thrown off his property. He sent Burns down to chase me off."

"No shit!" John reached for a cigarette. Matt watched him light it with trembling fingers. "No shit, he did that?"

"Yeah."

"Well, little brother, she's only a summer girl."

Matt shook his head. He kicked a beer can to the far end of the porch. "I'm not giving her up just because her father hates me."

John dragged on his cigarette. "Well, look at the two of us," he said. "Having a ball."

Matt pulled his arms out of the straps of his backpack and dropped it to the floor.

"Home for good?"

Matt looked at him, hearing something strange in his voice. "Yeah, I guess." He pushed the empty beer cans together with his foot. "Looks like I picked a good time to come home."

"Yeah, I guess you did," John said. He began to cry, at first only tears, but then, soon, loud sobs that shook his whole body.

Dumfounded, Matt stared down at him. John pressed his face into a cushion from the couch, but still the sobs came out, as if a wall had come tumbling down inside.

# Chapter 16

*T*hey sat up most of the night talking. This was something they had never done before.

Sometime during the small hours of the night, in the kitchen over cups of coffee that followed one another like compulsive potions to hold back sleep, they found themselves sharing a lot of secrets.

"I always hated Dad for dumping on you," John said. "I never could figure out what he had against you. I used to wonder if he'd find the same reason to hate me someday."

Matt nodded. His eyes were burned by the steam coming up from his coffee. "I don't think Dad hates me. He just doesn't love me very much."

"Yeah." John looked at his empty cigarette pack, then tossed it away. "But Mom, she loves you a lot."

"Too damn much. Feels like a big, wet marshmallow on top of me all the time, like she's afraid to let me grow up."

"It's crazy," John said, going after more coffee. "Dad never gave me time to be a kid."

"A lot of things are crazy," Matt said. "A lot of things in *this* family are crazy."

"But not us." John laughed. "Not us."

Matt shook his head. "Hell no, we're normal as apple pie."

"Mama's boy and wonder son," John said as he sat down again. "Super jock, winning the big game for dear old Dad. Do you have any idea how much I hated Little League? Do you have any idea how much I goddamn loathed it?"

Matt shook his head.

"Sure, how could you? Mom kept you out of it, wouldn't let you play, so you didn't have to . . ."

"I wanted to play," Matt told him. "I've envied you all my life. And . . . and hated you."

John looked at him. "I know . . ."

Outside, the first pale light was glowing in the eastern sky.

John rubbed his face. "I'm beat. And we still have two sides of the house to paint before they come home."

"We'll do it. We'll sleep for a couple of hours and then get up all raring to go. We're the apple-pie boys, remember?" Matt tried to laugh even though he felt tears in his eyes. "We can do anything."

On the way to the stairs, John turned to look at him. "I can't apologize for everything."

"Don't," Matt said. "To hell with it. I can't either."

\* \* \*

165

They got up at ten, dragging themselves out into the glare of the sunlight. All day, as they worked, Matt waited for the black Mercedes to drive up their street. Wouldn't Andrea find some way to get free today? Wouldn't she find some way to come tell him . . .

But she never came.

They painted until six o'clock, when the last square yard of clapboard had been covered twice. The house glowed in the late afternoon light.

"Well, there she is," John said. "A few places on the trim to fix, but we got it licked."

"And a whole day to spare."

"Piece of cake," John said. "Even with a dub . . ." He cut himself short. "Let's go out for supper."

They went downtown to Bob and Jerry's for a loaded pizza. When they got back to the house, Matt changed his clothes.

"I'm going to see Andrea."

"Want a ride?"

Matt shook his head. "I'll take my bike."

"Well, watch it. Don't let her old man catch you."

"I won't."

Matt rode out past the lake to the barrens. Despite the fact that he was so tired his eyes were on fire, he kept a sharp lookout for August Burns, ready to reverse his direction, hide in the woods, do whatever he had to do to avoid another confrontation with the constable.

August Burns was patrolling in some other part of town tonight. Matt abandoned the tarred road and hid his bike in a sumac grove. Under the pine trees it was

166

already dark, but out in the field the sky glow gave him a good view of the house. No lights showed yet in the windows.

He pushed away his fears as he approached the boathouse. Just because Andrea hadn't tried to see him today . . .

Someone had left the porch door ajar. Had he left it that way himself last night, in his rush to get away from August Burns? Insects had come inside during the day and buzzed now from one side of the porch to the other. He sat down in one of the chairs to wait for Andrea.

He was having a difficult time keeping his eyes open. Even the hard wooden chair he was sitting in didn't seem uncomfortable enough to keep him awake. Just before he fell asleep, he thought he saw something fly up from the edge of the lake: a bird much larger than a gull, beating its wings hard to gain altitude before gliding off toward the east.

He woke with a feeling of dread. It was late, much too late. Andrea had not come. He walked out onto the deck and looked up at the house. It was totally dark, at least from down here.

He climbed up through the field, over the top of the hill. There was no Mercedes in the drive.

At the front of the house the porch light was burning. It was the only light in all the darkness. Something white was pinned to the edge of the screen door.

He climbed the steps and tore the note down. He thought he knew already what it would say.

But he read it anyway:

*Dear Matt,*

*I wanted to see you before we left, but he's so insistent on going now and we'll be gone, I know, long before you finish painting for the day. I'll leave this note on the door. I'll leave the light on so you'll see it when you come up to find out what's happened.*

*Daddy is convinced he can't write here. His big poem is still unwritten. You remember the poem I told you about, the one he needs for the book coming out this winter?*

*So it's back to Boston, where he hopes to find it possible to write the poem.*

*I'm sorry he called the police to chase you away. He knew you were down there at the boathouse, but he never let on to me that he knew.*

*I'm going to miss you. We never said this to each other so I'll say it now. I love you.*

*Andrea*

And below, at the bottom of the sheet of paper, she had printed: I'LL WRITE.

He kept reading the note over and over again, as if somehow he might discover that he had read it incorrectly the first time.

He tried the door. It was locked. The porch light would have to go on burning, before an empty house, above an empty yard.

Going down the hill toward the boathouse, Matt carefully folded Andrea's note and placed it in his wallet. He did not go home. He sat alone on the deck for a long time, his back to the dark house up on the hill. Across the lake the little lights of Point Rollins glittered in the darkness. He watched them as if they might spell out some answer for him.

Then he stood up and walked to the beach and took off all his clothes, dropping them into a pile on the damp sand.

The water was cold, black, as uninviting as any bad dream that might steal its way into your sleep. He waded out slowly, the water creeping up his legs to his knees, to his thighs, to his waist.

For a moment he heard Andrea calling to him, urging him on with her encouragement, telling him he could do it, he could do it, if only he would try.

As he sank forward into the water, fear leaped up into his eyes like a little blue flame. It came down with him into the black water. His feet lifted, his hands went out before him.

He floated.

He gazed into the little blue flame. It began to shrink, to close in on itself around the edges. When his chest ached too much for him to hold his breath any longer, he brought his feet down toward the sand. Just for a moment he couldn't find his footing and the flame roared up as if to burn him to a cinder.

He drove his feet into the sand; he stood up. He saw the dark lake and the lights of Point Rollins, but the little blue flame was gone.

When he had caught his breath he floated again, to prove to himself that the first time was no fluke. Then he waded back onto the beach.

"I did it," he whispered aloud, to no one but the beach rocks and the grass. He shivered into his clothes and walked back into the woods to get his bike.

# Chapter 17

*H*is parents made connections to fly into Ellington, and he and John drove there to pick them up on the afternoon of the twenty-fifth of August. They had spent the morning cleaning the house, and yesterday they had touched up the trim. Hurt by Andrea's sudden departure with her father, Matt had wanted to work as hard as he could and had repainted far more of the trim than needed doing, while John stood below the ladder yelling at him to be careful.

"We could go on doing this forever," John said each time Matt came down off the ladder. "If you drip onto the white, we'll have to get that paint out again."

"I won't drip."

They moved the ladder and Matt went up again.

"What's the matter with you anyway?" John asked.

"Nothing."

"Bullshit. What's bugging you?"

"Andrea's gone."

"Summer girls fly south. Happens every year."

"Yeah."

"So you're drowning your sorrow in paint?"

"Something like that."

John finally took the brush away from him in disgust and washed it out. "Jesus, Matt, that's enough."

On the drive to Ellington, John talked about his upcoming year at college. "I'm going to throw everyone a curve, drop sports and study for a change."

Matt looked at him.

"I mean it. Maybe I'll try out for the cross-country ski team, something different like that. But they can take football and stick it sideways. I'm sick of getting my brains bashed in, what little I've got in that department."

Matt smiled. "What about all the locker-room groupies?"

"Never really liked them anyway. You have a big game, they're all over you. Go out there and stink, they forget they ever knew you."

John turned to look at him. "I'm serious, Matt. You think I can't change?"

Matt didn't answer right away. They were driving into the outskirts of Ellington before he nodded. "I hope you can."

The plane was late. He and John stood outside the tiny terminal, waiting by the fence.

"Excited they're coming home?" John asked.

Matt shook his head. "No, I'm not."

They looked at each other. "It can be different now," John said. "Because we both *know*."

The day before school started Matt rode out to the barrens in the evening, his field glasses around his neck. The sun, going down so much earlier now, was already behind the ridge as he walked the sandy roads under the pitch pines, through the small groves of gray birch trees.

The chickadees were still flitting about in the fading light, and a catbird whined in the bushes near the lake. He searched the treetops for his bird, the mystery bird, but if it was still around, it did not show itself.

When he came out beside the field, he told himself to turn back, but instead he walked up the hill to the Staffords' summer house. A recent rain had knocked down the flowers in the garden and eroded the gravel at the bottom of the drive.

The porch light still burned. Piles of scarlet leaves, early casualties from two maple trees in front of the house, were gathering by the steps. He kicked his way way through them and tried the door. It was still locked.

He gazed up at the black windows for a while and then returned down the long hill. He thought he was a silly fool for going there. Below him the lake stretched off to the east, cold and gray, and the boathouse with its sagging screens looked more derelict than ever.

His mother came to his room that night while he was looking through his unfinished journal wondering if it was worth the effort to race through it now, filling in all the missing entries.

"Matt?"

He turned toward her.

"What's troubling you?"

"Nothing."

"You're not yourself. What happened here this summer? I've never seen two people change so much as you and your brother have changed."

He shrugged.

"Is it because of that girl?"

Once he might have told her everything that had happened to him. Now he had no intention of telling her anything about Andrea. When she came up to his chair and tried to run her fingers over the back of his head, he ducked away.

"Matthew, I can tell when something's troubling my boy. I can always read you like a book."

"I'm not a book," he said.

"Matthew! I know that. I didn't mean . . ."

He brushed away her hands. " I'd like to be alone."

He heard her take in a sharp, short breath and hold it — something she always did when her feelings were hurt. He studied the last entry in his journal. He knew her eyes would be looking for his.

"This is my room, Mom. I'd like to be alone in it."

At the door she paused, and her voice when she spoke now was angry, snappish, trembling with emotion. "Seems to me you've always spent altogether too much time alone. It's not healthy. It's not normal."

If I'm not normal, he thought, then who's to blame for that? But aloud he said, "I'm fine."

"I have my doubts," she said on her way out.

She had always been able to frighten him with her

vague comments about his well-being. The world, after all, was full of terrible, unmentionable things that might hurt small boys, even boys who were not so small.

"Don't have doubts!" he shouted at her. "Don't bother having any doubts about me at all. I'm fine!"

Shouting was bound to bring his father into this, but he didn't care about that either.

"I'm fine," he repeated softly to himself.

He turned in his journal the way it was, and he was not surprised when Mr. Doninger, his science teacher, asked him to stay at the end of biology class Friday.

"What happened, Matt?" Mr. Doninger demanded. He rapped his fingers hard on the top cover of the journal. "It's great for starters, then blam — it just stops." He peered across his desk. "It just stops."

"I know. I got distracted."

"Scientists don't get distracted." Mr. Doninger was clearly upset. "How can I give you any extra credit for this?"

"I'm sorry," Matt said. The next class was filing in and he was eager to get away. "It's okay about the extra credit because I know I don't deserve it. But I'm still interested in birds. I'm still observing."

Mr. Doninger ran his fingers through his thinning hair. "And what's this nonsense about seeing a painted bunting? You know they don't come this far north."

Matt nodded. "I couldn't positively identify it. I think I say somewhere in there that it was probably an escaped pet."

"Was probably?" Mr. Doninger echoed.

"Well, I just don't know."

Mr. Doninger stood up and told his class to be quiet. He scribbled out a pass so that Matt could get into his next class and handed it to him along with the unfinished journal. "Well, Matt, I'm sorry you got distracted. The journal was good as far as it went. You've always been a student I expect to amount to something someday." He followed Matt to the door. "Get back on track, will you?"

Matt nodded and went out into the corridor. The apple-pie boys were still not doing so great, he thought, remembering the look on John's face as he went out the door with Dad on his way back to college. Dad had talked about football for a solid week before it was time for John to leave. John had said nothing about not going out for the team.

Matt checked the mail on his way home. There was still no letter from Andrea.

By the middle of September the porch light at the Staffords' house had burned out. He went there occasionally, when his feet, of their own accord, took him that way through the woods. He wrote Andrea a letter and mailed it to Boston. He had no street address to put on the envelope but thought he might get lucky. The letter came back in a week, undelivered, officially rejected by the post office, with various purple-inked stampings on it to prove they had tried. He had an inspiration then and copied down the address of Stark Stafford's publisher from *Sound Side*. He put the letter into a fresh new envelope and sent it off care of the publisher.

At least this time it didn't come back. But Andrea didn't answer it, either.

He wrote her again early in October, vaguely encouraged by the fact that the first letter had not come back, that it had been delivered to someone. He told her he missed her. He told her the weather was getting cold, the trees were already a blaze of autumn colors. He told her he was signing up for swimming lessons.

This letter disappeared into the great unknown, too, and brought no return letter from her. After that, he just thought about her a lot.

The swimming course was going to be taught at the college gym up in Audenville, one night a week, starting the third week of October. Anyone could sign up for it, provided he or she had the twenty-five dollars. Matt took the money from his savings account and rode up to Audenville on his bike one afternoon after school, through a swirl of leaves blowing from the maple trees that lined the road.

At the gym he wandered around looking for someone who knew something about the swimming course, and finally found a girl behind a desk in the community-center room who said she'd be glad to take his money and add his name to the list.

"Matt Zaharis," he told her.

She looked up.

"Z-a-h-a-r-i-s."

She gave him a receipt and a brochure describing the course. "The first class is Wednesday night, at seven."

She was pretty; she looked a little like Andrea. He

caught himself staring at her. "Are you teaching the course?" he asked.

She shook her head. "Connie Randolph is. She's mentioned in the brochure. She's very qualified."

He found a bench out in the corridor and read the brochure from front to back. Then he went to look at the pool. It shimmered wet and green in a large barn of a room behind the basketball court. He stared at it until someone asked him what he wanted, then he ducked away and found a pay telephone. His hands were trembling slightly as he dialed the number he had found in the brochure, Connie Randolph's number, which you could call in case you had to cancel at the last minute and wanted a partial rebate of your money.

A husky voice answered on the fourth ring. "Yes?"

"Connie Randolph?"

"Yes, who is this?"

"My name is Matt Zaharis. I just signed up for your swimming course and I . . ."

"Yes, Mr. Zaharis?" she asked while he was stumbling over his question. "The first class is Wednesday night at seven, as you could have found out by reading the brochure."

"That's not why I'm calling."

"Exactly why are you calling, Mr. Zaharis?"

He wiped the sweat out of his eyes. "I've always been afraid of the water. This summer I . . . this summer I got to the point where I could go in and float and not be so afraid I'd panic or anything like that, but I'm still not exactly relaxed about it, but I intend . . ." He took a deep breath. "I intend to try very hard. Not to be afraid," he said.

There was a long silence on the other end of the line. "You said you can float?"

"Yes."

"On your own?"

"Yes."

"Then I don't see that there should be any problem, Mr. Zaharis. It's not so unusual a problem. I mean, if everyone could swim already, we wouldn't be offering a course for nonswimmers, now would we?"

"No, I guess not." Relief washed over him. He tried to pick up his extra change, dropping most of it on the floor.

"Does that answer your question, Mr. Zaharis?"

"Yes, it does. I just wanted you to know that I intend to try very hard."

"I'm sure you will, Mr. Zaharis. See you Wednesday night."

After she hung up, he retrieved his change from the floor. On his way out to the parking lot he passed the community-center room. He couldn't resist leaning in and waving to the girl behind the desk.

"It's all set," he called to her. "It's going to be okay."

She looked at him blankly for a moment, but then she said she was glad everything was working out all right.

The night before his first swimming class he had a dream about the mystery bird. He dreamed it was winter. His feet squeaked on the thin layer of snow that covered the sandy roads in the pine barrens. As he walked toward the lake, his breath formed a white cloud before his face. Something fluttered down from the top of a pine tree. He ran forward and found the brightly colored bird lying dead in the snow. When he bent down to pick it up, the colors faded; and what he finally held in his hands was only an ordinary sparrow, its feathers drab brown and gray, nothing more.

The dream stayed with him all day at school. Two of his teachers complained about his lack of attention. After school he packed his new swim trunks and towel in his brother's old gym bag.

"You won't expect too much, will you?" his mother cautioned him during his early supper.

"I'll be okay," he told her.

She obviously was not convinced by this. As he pulled on his jacket, she followed him to the door. "Let me drive you up there," she said.

"I'll ride my bike."

On the side steps they were caught in a cold gust of wind.

"You'll freeze," she complained.

"No, I won't."

On the long ride up to Audenville he bent low over the handlebars, trying to make a small target for the wind. He kept thinking about the dream, about the way the bird had lost its colors.

At the college gym he changed with the other men in the locker room. Connie Randolph had a loud voice at poolside, but she seemed to know what she was doing.

She had them all show what they could do. He floated. "Very good, Mr. Zaharis," she told him. "Very good."

The first lesson went well. He didn't disappoint himself. There were twenty other people in his class, and he liked some of them.

When he got home, he wrote John a letter all about it and mailed it the next morning on his way to school. Under the weekly circular from Antonio's Market in their mailbox, there was a card from Andrea.

# Chapter 18

*O*n the front of the postcard was a picture of the Boston skyline at night, towers of light above the harbor. On the back Andrea had written:

> *Matt,*
>     *I'm coming Saturday the 24th to close up the house. I should arrive by noon. Can you meet me there?*
>
> > *Love,*
> > *Andrea*

He read the card twice. He carefully placed it in the middle of his math book, but he had it out again before he reached school.

The twenty-fourth was this coming Saturday, just two days away. At first this seemed no time at all, so immediate was the change her card brought with it. But by the middle of his morning study hall the two days loomed up before him like a big slice of forever.

Some of his classmates were going to watch the football team scrimmage with Wilson Prep that afternoon after school. He made up an excuse to skip the game and walked home the long way, through the yellow and gold leaves drifting down from the trees that lined the streets below Oak Hill. There was a place near the top of the hill where he could sit and look out over the whole town. He went there now and sat until dark.

When he came into the house through the side door, his mother looked up from the chopping block in the kitchen and asked him where he had been all afternoon. He told her he had been abducted by terrorists but had managed to ditch them when they stopped at the Laundromat to telephone Beirut.

"Matt, be serious."

"I am."

She stared at him. "Did you pick up the mail?"

He nodded. "There was just a circular from Antonio's. I pitched it."

At supper he played with his food. He had no appetite at all.

"Don't you feel well?" his mother asked, reaching over to touch his forehead.

He pulled away from her hand. "I'm fine."

"Then wipe that stupid grin off your face and eat your supper," his father said.

"Yes, sir."

As soon as he could, Matt excused himself and went up to his room, where he spent the rest of the night imagining things.

Saturday morning came gray with rain clouds. By ten o'clock a mist had turned all the colored leaves to neon shades of red and yellow. By ten-thirty Matt couldn't wait any longer. He slipped out of the house while his mother was busy on the telephone. As he wheeled his bike from the garage, he saw her looking out the window at him, the telephone against her shoulder. He waved and rode quickly away.

The streets were mirrors of the glaring clouds. Beside the lake most of the boats had been hauled up and put under cover, the sandy beaches empty now except for stray weekend visitors out for determined walks in the wet weather. They looked toward the lake as if to spot the first signs of winter ice, as if afraid a sudden cold snap might trap them here until spring.

Matt smelled wood fires burning: sweet birch and acrid half-dried oak. From the chimneys of some of the cottages smoke drifted up into the rain.

He could still taste the coffee he had gulped this morning with his breakfast toast. It threatened never to settle down. As he turned onto Westerly Road, he skidded on a patch of wet leaves plastered to the pavement and fell over. More slowly then he pedaled the rest of the way to Gunfire.

He had foolishly hoped she might already be there, having come early because she couldn't stick patiently to *her* schedule. Up to the very last moment he looked for the black Mercedes.

But Gunfire was still deserted. He pulled his bike onto the front porch and sat on the steps among the leaves that had gathered there all fall. It was probably eleven by now and he would have to wait for at least an hour.

He had her postcard with him, and he looked at it while he waited. Fortunately the words had not been worn off by frequent reading. The picture of the Boston skyline came in for its share of study. He was still imagining a lot of things; sometimes his face grew warm from his thoughts and he would leave the shelter of the porch to walk across the yard in the mist, holding his face up to the cool, fine droplets of rain.

After a while a terrible thought pounced on him like a tiger from the darkness in the back of his mind, where perhaps it had lain in wait for him since the arrival of her card: What if Andrea brought her father?

He pulled out the card and read it again. She did not say she was coming alone; he had only assumed she was. But wouldn't she tell him if she were bringing her father? Wouldn't she caution him to wait at the boathouse?

He walked up the drive and back again, resolutely refusing to allow himself to take her postcard one more time from his dry back pocket. But it was not a day to put away doubts confidently. They paced over the gravel with him; they hung about his head like a smoky cloud.

She was late. Even without a watch he had to admit this eventually. He listened for the sound of car tires on the wet pavement of Westerly Road. Whenever a car approached the house he looked up hopefully, then watched in gray despair as it drove by.

There were a dozen reasons why she might be late, but there was also the one thought that perhaps she

wasn't coming. He had a sudden picture of himself waiting there all afternoon in the rain until night fell and
buried him together with his hopes, together with his
secret imaginings: one big aching lump under the thick
clouds of a rainy fall night.

This was too much. Leaving his bike on the porch to
let her know he was there if she came while he was gone,
he ran along the drive to the edge of the hill and then
down through the tall, wet grass to the boathouse at the
lakeside. Here he paced the deck, at least safe from the
torment of the cars that passed on Westerly Road, that
passed and passed and never turned out to be *her* car,
never rolled into the drive beside Gunfire with happy,
urgent, blaring horns.

A wet breeze was blowing off the lake. It fluttered by
the porch screens, then died in the field where the tall
grass sagged under the weight of the rain. But further
up the hill, near the garden . . .

"Matt!"

He saw her the moment she called to him, as she came
over the top of the hill, as she started to run down through
the grass toward him. He did not realize he was running
too, until he felt the wet tangle of the grass around his legs.

Halfway down the hill she fell. By the time she had
regained her feet, he was there beside her and saw her
glistening face and the smile that was the brightest spot
in all that gray landscape.

"Matt, I'm sorry I'm . . ."

He grabbed her plaid jacket and pulled her tight. She
smelled of herbal shampoo and car leather and wet wool.
Her lips tasted salty.

186

"Were you worried?" she asked when they stepped back to look at each other.

"No, I . . ." His lie faltered as he looked into her eyes. "Yeah, I was."

She took his hand and began pulling him up the hill. "Oh, the traffic was awful and I got a late start and I stopped to pick up some groceries."

At the top of the hill she turned again to face him. Her plaid jacket was wet from her fall in the grass, her dark hair was down over her eyes.

"Can you help me put up the storm shutters?" she asked.

He nodded.

"Even in this rain?"

He nodded again. "Anything you'd like to do," he said.

# Chapter 19

*H*e helped her carry the two bags of groceries into the house from the car. Inside, the rooms were chilly and damp, with a moldy smell that had gathered there since the last day the windows had been open to the sunny summer.

"The porch light went out," he told her. "Burned out, unless you had the power shut off."

She shook her head and flicked a wall switch in the kitchen. The overhead light snapped on, burning wanly in the washed-out daylight that came through the windows.

"You found the note, then," she said, beginning to unpack the food.

"Yeah, I did."

"Did you hate me?"

Again he couldn't lie. "For a while."

"Poor Matt," she said. She had a carton of eggs and a package of bacon in her hands. The smile on her lips looked oddly patched on. "Do you still hate me?"

He shook his head. He helped her put away the food. In the refrigerator they found several strange remains from summer.

Andrea went to the side door and pulled it open. While she stood there watching, he fought his way through the fumes, grabbing everything that had gone bad and throwing it into one of the empty grocery bags. This he finally took outside and deposited in the garbage can below the side steps. Andrea was still standing by the open door.

"The smell will clear out in a while," he told her as he came back inside. He looked at all the food still waiting to be put away. "You brought a lot."

"Well, you're staying for supper, aren't you?"

"I'd like to."

"I'll cook us a couple of great steaks and we'll build a fire and . . ." She stopped suddenly. "God, I've missed you."

They left the rest of the food on the table, left the refrigerator open to air out. Andrea uncorked a bottle of wine and brought it with her into the front room. They sipped from it as they carried in wood from outside for the fire later.

"It's so wet," she said. "Do you think we can get it to burn?"

He nodded. "We'll find some dry wood to start it." He put down his armload of logs. "I was afraid your father might come with you."

"He wanted to. I made a bargain with him."

"What kind of bargain?"

She looked away. "Just a . . . bargain." She picked up the wine bottle, took a sip, then handed it to him "I wrote you a dozen letters."

"I didn't get any."

"I know. I tore them all up."

He wondered if she could guess what these letters would have meant to him during the fall. "Why did you?"

She shrugged. Taking the wine bottle back, she tilted it up and drank. She wiped her mouth on her sleeve. "They just weren't right, somehow."

"What do you mean?"

She shook her head impatiently. "They just weren't right. I kept thinking I could find a better way to say things."

They stared at each other. To break the silence, he said, "I wrote you, too. One letter came back because I didn't have your full address. So then I sent it care of your father's publisher, and another letter a couple weeks after that."

He hadn't meant to hurt her in return, but the pain showed on her face. "To Cambrian House?" she asked softly. "I never got them."

"Your father probably made sure you didn't," Matt said.

"Maybe Cambrian never forwarded them."

"Maybe." He was suddenly angry. He looked away. "Glad you sent the card, anyway."

"Me too," she said. She touched his arm. "Come on, let's get those shutters up before the rain gets any harder."

It took them most of the afternoon to put up the shutters.

The ladder was slippery and the shutters awkward in the wind that blew from the lake.

"Who took them down in the first place?" Matt asked as they sorted through the piles, trying to match the correct set of shutters to each window.

Andrea pushed back her hair, leaving a smudge on her forehead. "The man who owned the house before us was going to have them scraped and painted. He sold the place to us first."

Matt started back up the ladder. "I'll paint them for you next year," he told her. "I work cheap."

She didn't answer. When he looked down at her, she was staring at her finger.

"Splinter?"

She shook her head. "It's nothing."

They worked as quickly as they could, hanging the shutters on the old hinges still mounted beside each window. They fastened the shutters with long screws, top and bottom, driving the screws into the tired holes with a bent screwdriver that had a perverse habit of slipping out of Matt's hand to bury itself in the muddy ground below. In the middle of the afternoon, Andrea ducked inside to put away the food before it spoiled. She came back with a couple of ham sandwiches and a can of Coke.

They munched hungrily under the dubious shelter of the ladder. The rain, after stopping for a while, was now falling all the harder. Darkness was coming early, hanging in gray streaks from the low clouds.

"Now admit it," Andrea said, licking mustard off her fingers. "You have lots of good times with me, don't you?"

He laughed. "This *is* a good time," he said.

"Bullshit."

"It is."

She looked at him. "You're a sweetheart, you know?"

"You're the only person who thinks so."

"Well, who else counts?"

He smiled. "No one else."

They finished the Coke and went back to work. Some of the windows didn't have shutters. They raced into town in the Mercedes before the hardware store closed, and bought a caulking gun and two tubes of caulking compound. Back at the house they sealed the cracks around the shutterless windows to keep out the winter weather.

"Now the boathouse and we're done," Andrea said.

He looked at her. "The boathouse?" He brushed rain off his eyebrows.

She nodded. "There are sheets of plywood that go on the boathouse windows. Otherwise the snow will get in and . . ."

"Okay, let's go."

She got the key from inside the house and they walked down through the field. Matt's sweat shirt was soaked by now, sagging halfway to his knees. From inside the storage area of the boathouse, where an old rowboat now lay in ruin, they dragged out several sheets of gray, warped plywood. It took them all the rest of the afternoon to nail these up over the porch windows.

"I'm tired," Andrea moaned when they were finally done. Her plaid jacket was covered with streaks of dirt from the plywood. Her hair lay flattened against her forehead. While she was closing and locking the door to the storage area, Matt looked out at the lake. He was already soaked to the skin. It wouldn't hurt now to go ahead and do what he had suddenly realized he wanted to do.

"Coming?"

"I want to show you something." He grabbed her hand and pulled her along the path toward the beach.

"What are you doing, Matt?" she complained. "I'm cold and I'm tired and I want to get dried off and . . ." She stopped when she realized he was pulling off his clothes. "Matt, are you crazy?"

He unbuttoned his inside shirt and kicked off his jeans. "Just watch." He waded into the water. It was so cold he wouldn't have been surprised to find cakes of ice drifting in with the wind. When he had waded out far enough, he launched himself into a forward float. After a few seconds he rolled over onto his back and floated *that* way, as he had learned to do during his first swimming lesson last Wednesday night.

When he stood up, water ran down into his eyes from his hair and he could barely see her in the fading light. "Well, what do you think?" he shouted. "Is there a future for me on the Olympic team?"

She met him at the water's edge and wrapped her jacket around him. He couldn't tell if she was crying or if it was just the rain glistening all over her face.

"You *are* crazy," she said.

"Yeah, but at least I don't sink anymore." He told her about his swimming class as they gathered up his clothes and ran up the hill to the house. In the kitchen she kissed him.

"Proud of me, aren't you?"

"Maybe."

"Come on, admit it. Blew your socks off, didn't I?"

"Maybe."

He was shivering, standing in a puddle of water that was forming on the kitchen floor at his feet.

"You'll catch cold," she said, and went looking for dry clothes.

While she was upstairs, he went into the front room and wrapped himself in a blanket from the couch. Then he crumpled up some newspaper and placed it between the andirons in the fireplace. In the cellar he found a pile of old boards. He brought up all the pieces he could carry. This dry wood caught fire quickly; gradually he began putting the wet logs on top of the flames. They hissed for a while, but by carefully adding more dry wood as needed he slowly built up a blaze that could keep itself going.

He was still fussing with the fire when Andrea came down.

"There's no end to your talents," she said. She had brushed her hair and put on a flannel robe. She held another robe out for him. "A gift from the former occupants. They left a ton of things up in the attic."

The robe smelled of dust and mothballs, but it was dry. As he pulled it on she unfolded a wooden rack and they hung up their wet clothes to dry in front of the fire.

In the kitchen he watched her prepare a salad. "How late can you stay?" she asked, carefully slicing the tomatoes.

He watched the pieces of tomato fall to the side of the knife blade. "I'm not going home tonight," he said.

She didn't look up. "What about your parents?"

"I'll call home later, so they won't worry."

She laughed. "Oh, they'll worry."

He shrugged, picking up a piece of carrot and biting off the end. "They'll survive."

She glanced up at him. He was surprised to see that her face had flushed to a warm shade of pink. "You're sure?" she asked.

He nodded. "Yes, I'm sure."

He broiled the steaks in the bottom of the gas stove while she sliced the bread and put it in the oven to heat. In the dining room she lit four candles, two at each end of the table. From the front room they could hear the warm sound of the fire crackling its way through the wood. Their wine glasses sparkled in the candlelight.

He raised his glass. "To Andrea," he said. He tried to think of something brilliant to say but nothing came to him. "To Andrea," he said again.

She sipped her wine. "Did you ever get a chance to read *Sound Side?*"

He nodded.

"And?"

"I didn't enjoy it as much as the early poems, like 'A Winter's Eve.' "

She looked angry. "That's what all the reviewers said."

"Maybe they were right."

195

"Maybe they just get their kicks tearing down great writers like my father." Her hand was trembling as she put down her glass.

"Has he written his big poem?"

"No."

"That's too bad," Matt said, wondering if he really meant it. He didn't want to talk about her father, but they seemed stuck on the subject.

"The book will be published as is," Andrea told him.

"Without the big poem?"

"Yes."

They ate slowly. When Matt came back from putting more wood on the fire, he unwrapped another slice of bread for each of them. "Will your father miss you this weekend?" he asked.

She nodded. "I imagine so."

"But you came anyway."

"Yes, I did." She cut up her last piece of steak. "The house has to be closed, the water pipes drained." She looked across the table at him, then looked back at her plate. "We're going away for a while."

He put down his wine glass. Making his voice as casual as he could, he asked, "Where to?"

She stared over his shoulder. "Portugal, Spain, Italy, perhaps a few places a bit more exotic than that. It depends."

"On what?"

"How the articles go. Daddy's agreed to write a series of travel pieces for a new magazine."

"And you're going with him?"

She nodded. "Yes, I am."

"Was that your bargain?" He tried to chew his way through another piece of steak, but it was suddenly tough and dry. "Well," he said. "Guess you must be excited."

She didn't answer him. They cleared the table, bringing everything back into the kitchen. "We won't be gone forever, you know," she said. "It's not like forever."

He searched for the dishrag. "I guess it just feels like it might be," he said.

She snatched the dishrag away from him and began savagely wiping the stove. "What would make more sense? For me to leave him and come up here and clerk in a drugstore while you finish school?"

He didn't answer her.

"That would make sense, wouldn't it, Matt? Maybe we could go to your senior prom together."

"That's not what I meant."

"Then what did you mean?"

He shrugged. "I don't know."

Returning to the sink she said, "I'll do the dishes."

He took back the dishrag. "No, you dry. I hate to dry dishes."

The telephone at the house wasn't working. His clothes were still damp but he put them on anyway. "There's a telephone booth down by the town beach," he told her. "I can call from there."

Still in her robe she drove him to the beach, then waited in the car while he made his call. His mother answered. When he said hello, he heard her take her quick, sharp breath.

"Matt! Where are you?"

"In a phone booth."

"What's wrong? What's happening to you? It's late, we're . . ."

"I'm fine," he cut in. "Look, I'm not coming home tonight, and I just didn't want you and Dad to worry, so I'm calling to . . ."

"What do you mean, you're not coming home?" she demanded. Her voice was getting higher. In the distance he could hear his father shouting something to her.

"I won't be home tonight," he repeated. "I'll be home sometime tomorrow. So don't worry about me."

"Matthew!"

His father's voice was getting louder. "Good-bye," Matt said quickly and hung up.

Outside the booth the wind blew cold against his damp clothes. The clouds were drifting away, opening up spaces for the icy, glittering stars. In the car Andrea had the heat going.

"How did they take it?" she asked.

He laughed, but it wasn't a very hearty, happy sound. "They're furious."

"You can still change your mind," she said softly.

"No way."

She backed into the road and turned the car through the intersection. Her hand slipped off the wheel and into his. They drove back to the house in silence.

The fire had dwindled down to glowing coals, but the rest of the wood had dried out a bit by now. He soon had the flames roaring again. Andrea insisted he get out of his damp clothes and back into the robe. They sat on the couch together in front of the fire, finishing the bottle of wine from dinner. She held his hand in her lap.

"Someday I *will* leave him," she said. "But I can't yet." She looked at him as if she hoped to see some sign of understanding on his face.

"Will you be back next summer?" he asked. "Will you come up here?"

She opened the fingers of his hand, closed them again. "I don't know," she said.

When the wine was gone, they let the fire burn low and then they went upstairs to her room. She turned down the covers, then disappeared into the bathroom. Her windows were two of the ones that had no shutters, and he could hear the wind blowing outside, tearing the last of the leaves from the trees.

"Get in," she said when she came back from the bathroom. "Don't stand here in the cold."

She had put on a long cotton gown that came all the way to her feet. Just the same, she shivered when she touched the cold sheets.

They were together for a long while, and at one point she cried, "I don't ever want to leave you." She dug her fingers into his shoulders as if it were some force from outside, perhaps the wind, that was going to pull them apart. "I'll stay," she cried, "I'll stay, I'll stay . . ."

But later, sitting on the edge of the bed, gazing down at him, she said, "I'll send you the most wonderful letters, you'll see. I'll write about everything I do. It will be just like you're there. You'll see."

When the light was out, he lay awake for a long time.

Outside, the wind was blowing hard, working on a shutter that they had not fastened tightly enough, banging it against the side of the house. In the morning they would have to find it, to fasten it again.

He lay beside her in the dark and listened to the wind for hours; and when he finally slept, the wind came into his dreams; a vast rush of air, a moving sky.

He woke with a start. Andrea stirred beside him. "What is it?" she asked, her voice low and sleepy.

"Nothing, just a dream," he told her.

He closed his eyes again and drifted back into sleep and dreamed he was a bird, his colors bright and clean, his wings so broad and strong they never tired. He flew on the wind, upon the rushing air. The sky moved with him; the green hills slipped away forever behind him. All night long he dreamed of the bird flying from home.